"I don't relationsh_____ship, David."

"I know." He brushed his thumb along her jaw. "I've been wanting to do that for a long time," he said, soft and gruff.

"You have?"

"Yeah."

"Please don't fire me."

He dropped his hand. "I have no intention of firing you."

"You can't sleep with me, either. We can't go there at all. We can't kiss again. I can't lose this job, David. I can't."

His gaze held steady. "Can you forget this happened?"

"I have to."

Dear Reader,

Writers are often asked where we get our ideas. The answer is both simple and complicated. Inspiration comes from everywhere—observations, dreams, fantasies and experience. Most stories are combinations of all the elements.

My new series, WIVES FOR HIRE, is no exception. In each book, I explore the connection of three brothers who aren't looking for love then find it where they least expect. I have three brothers, and so I've observed the connection between them all my life and enjoy how they like each other as well as love each other. Jibes and jabs are a big part of the sibling relationship, but so is unconditional support.

And when a man falls in love, his brothers will tease and question and congratulate. It's all part of being a brother.

That's what I want to explore in this series—each man finding the woman of his dreams, and the joy of having brothers, someone you can count on for your entire life, who has a history with you that no one else has.

I hope you enjoy learning about the Falcon brothers and their loves. Watch for the second book of the series, *The Single Dad's Virgin Wife,* available in October.

Happy reading,

Susan

THE BACHELOR'S STAND-IN WIFE

SUSAN CROSBY

SPECIAL EDITION®

Published by Silhouette Books

America's Publisher of Contemporary Romance

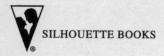

SILHOUETTE BOOKS

ISBN-13: 978-0-373-24912-1
ISBN-10:   0-373-24912-8

THE BACHELOR'S STAND-IN WIFE

Printed in U.S.A.

Books by Susan Crosby

Silhouette Special Edition

The Bachelor's Stand-In Wife #1912

Silhouette Desire

Christmas Bonus, Strings Attached #1554
†*Private Indiscretions* #1570
†*Hot Contact* #1590
†*Rules of Attraction* #1647
†*Heart of the Raven* #1653
†*Secrets of Paternity* #1659
The Forbidden Twin #1717
Forced to the Altar #1733
Bound by the Baby #1797

*Wives for Hire
†Behind Closed Doors

SUSAN CROSBY

believes in the value of setting goals, but also in the magic of making wishes, which often do come true—as long as she works hard enough. Along life's journey she's done a lot of the usual things—married, had children, attended college a little later than the average coed and earned a B.A. in English. Then she dove off the deep end into a full-time writing career, a wish come true.

Susan enjoys writing about people who take a chance on love, sometimes against all odds. She loves warm, strong heroes and good-hearted, self-reliant heroines, and will always believe in happily ever after.

More can be learned about her at www.susancrosby.com.

To Gail Chasan with gratitude, for the long-time support
and enthusiasm, then and now.
Thank you for the wonderful opportunities.

And to Sandra Dark, my wordy friend,
who proves the statement, "Writers write." You do it well.

Chapter One

David Falcon dragged his hands down his face as a woman took a seat across the desk from him.

"Well?" she asked.

"What's to think about? I just interviewed my twelfth candidate in two days, and I finally realized I'm delusional to hope I can find someone who fits my needs." He tipped his chair back to look at Denise Watson, the efficient, thirty-something director of At Your Service, a prestigious domestic-and-clerical-help agency nicknamed by many clients as "Wives for Hire." They were seated in her interview room.

"If you have to compromise on something, what would it be?" Denise asked.

He'd been doing a lot of compromising lately—for three years, in fact. He wasn't interested in more of the same. "I'm not giving up on the ideal yet. You've got other candidates, right?"

"One."

"That's all?"

"From my own staffing pool. As you pointed out, you have specific and complex needs. I'd be happy to advertise and screen them for you."

"What are your thoughts about the one remaining?"

She set a folder on the desk in front of him and smiled. "I've learned not to second-guess the client."

He half smiled in return. "Send her in, please." He skimmed the woman's résumé. Ten years' experience as a domestic, seven in clerical jobs. He speculated on her age—midthirties to forty, maybe? There were too many questions he wasn't allowed to ask legally, tying his hands, leaving him only intuition and guesswork about her age. He was twenty-nine. It was critical that she be older than him.

"Hello. I'm Valerie Sinclair," came a quiet but level voice.

He looked up. The woman was either extraordinarily well preserved or had lied about her work experience. She didn't look a day over twenty-five. She wore a dress and jacket that was way too formal and warm for a hot August day in Sacramento, as if trying to look older. And her hair, a rich, shiny color, like chestnuts, was bundled up in some kind of bun or whatever that style was called, but couldn't take away from her young age. Her eyes were hazel and direct. No rings on her slender fingers; her nails were short, clean and unpolished.

"I'm David Falcon. Please, have a seat," he said, wondering how she'd passed At Your Service's background check. She had to have lied—

To hell with the law, he decided. If she could lie about her work experience, he could ask the questions he wanted to. "How old are you, Ms. Sinclair?"

She stiffened. "I'm twenty-six."

"How is it you have seventeen years of work experience? You started working when you were nine?"

"Eight, actually. Not legally, of course, but my mother has

been housekeeper for a family in Palm Springs since I was five. I was put to work early."

"Doing what?"

"In the beginning, dusting and sweeping. New responsibilities were added as I could handle them."

"Your mother allowed you to be used like that?"

"Used?" She smiled slightly. "Didn't you do chores as a child? The family wasn't in residence full-time. We lived on-site. It was my home."

David didn't know what to think. On the one hand it seemed that child labor laws were violated. On the other, her point was well taken—*to* a point. "Did you receive a salary?"

"An allowance from my mother, which increased as my responsibilities did. I don't think it's worth a lot of discussion, Mr. Falcon. My understanding is that you're looking for someone to run your household and also be your administrative assistant. I listed the domestic work so that you would know I had a lot of experience in that field."

David studied her. She was...soothing, he decided. Her feathers didn't ruffle easily.

"May I ask the nature of your business?" she asked.

"My brother and I own Falcon Motorcars."

"I've never heard of that make."

"They're custom-made. Our clients aren't the average car buyers, so we don't need to advertise. Most buyers are European, which is why I've been out of the country more than I've been home the past few years. Which is also why I'm looking for someone to take charge of things here, personally and professionally."

"Denise said you want a live-in."

A wife without the sex was what he wanted. Someone experienced, efficient and of a certain age. "That's a requirement. Is that a problem?"

"Not at all."

"Given the time difference between California and the continent, you might be awakened during the night to take care of business for me, or work until midnight, or get up at four."

"I can do that."

"How are your computer skills?"

"Denise tested me on five different programs. I assume the results are in my folder."

He found the report and read it, letting her wait, testing her patience. She didn't fidget. "Why did you leave your last job?"

"Sexual harassment." She said it as easily as she might have said she'd gone to the grocery store.

He flattened his hands on top of the folder. "Did you file suit?"

Again that slight smile touched her lips. "*I* was accused of sexual harassment."

David looked her over once more. Was that the reason for the buttoned-up outfit she wore? Beneath it was a slender, attractive body, he could tell. And maybe with her hair down and some makeup on, she would look sexy. She didn't want to look sexy? "Were you guilty?"

"Quite the opposite."

He let that information sink in. "He was harassing you?"

She nodded once, sharply, the only outward indication of how much the situation bothered her.

"Why didn't you report him?"

"I did. That's when he turned it around to me instead. Look, it's dead and buried for me."

"Is it? I would imagine it's followed you and made it difficult to find a job," he said, knowing how such things worked.

She hesitated, then gave a taut smile.

Pride. He understood it all too well. "Let me share my recent experiences," he said. "My last housekeeper stole from me. My last four administrative assistants left because of pregnancy or child-care-related issues, each of them at just about the time they were fully trained. Frankly, I'd pretty much decided this time around to hire a woman beyond child-bearing age. You don't fit that qualification."

Her stark disappointment flashed, but he couldn't let that interfere with his decision-making process. "As much as I'd like to hire you—"

His cell phone rang. He would've ignored it, except it was his brother Noah, the only caller David couldn't ignore. "Excuse me a moment," he said, then left the room.

Valerie waited for David Falcon to shut the door before she closed her eyes. *As much as I'd like to hire you.* His mind was apparently made up. Her hands shook; her mouth went dry. She was at the end of her already short rope. If she didn't get this job she didn't know what she was going to do. She'd used every penny of her meager savings. Her credit card was maxed out. How could she convince him to hire her?

She was *this* close to being homeless, although a homeless shelter might be better than the apartment complex where she lived, in a part of town where drive-by shootings weren't uncommon. This job would mean a steady income and a safe place to live. For her and—

"Sorry about that," David said, returning. "As I started to say, as much as I'd like to hire you, given your job skills, I'm hesitant. I would need your assurance that you won't be taking off to get married anytime soon. I need to know you're not pregnant or intending to get pregnant anytime soon. I would be hiring you to take care of *me*—my house and my business—not a baby."

Valerie clenched her hands. She still had a chance. *Say the right thing. Say the right thing.* "I'm not even dating anyone, so the issue of marriage is nonexistent. Which would also, therefore, mean no pregnancy or babies in sight. However, I do have a daughter, Hannah. She's eight." Valerie saw his eyes dull with disappointment. "She's a quiet, obedient child, I promise you."

She waited for lightning to strike her for the fib, then continued to plead her case. "My daughter doesn't require the care that a baby does. You won't even know she's there."

Valerie had her own reasons for not letting Hannah get close to him, anyway. "Just give me a chance to prove myself," she said, trying not to beg.

He leaned back in his chair, his gaze never leaving hers. She didn't look away, either. *Please hire me. Please.*

"Let's try it for a month," he said at last.

Emotions tumbled through the desert of what her life had become. She couldn't even speak.

"I'll pay your rent for where you're living now so that you have a place to go back to if it doesn't work out."

She wouldn't move back to that hellhole under any circumstances. She swallowed against the still roiling emotions. "It's not necessary. I was going to look for a new place anyway."

"All right. You'll be living in a cottage behind the main house, and it's fully furnished, including all the kitchen things. I'll arrange for some movers and a storage unit for your belongings."

A cottage? Their own space? "My apartment came furnished. I have very little to transport." She and Hannah had moved so many times, they had the routine down pat.

"You're making this very easy, Ms. Sinclair."

"Valerie. It's my job to make your life easy."

"If you can pull that off, you're a miracle worker."

He stood; she did, as well. Apparently when he made up his mind, that was that.

"How soon can you start?" he asked.

"Where is your house?"

"In Chance City, close to Grass Valley and Nevada City. Are you familiar with the area?"

"Not much. I know it's a Mother Lode location from the gold rush era."

"Right. It's beautiful country, but the house itself is a little isolated."

"Isolation doesn't bother me." They would be about an hour north of Sacramento. Clean air, and stars at night. Trees. *Their own cottage.* "I can be there tonight."

"I'll send someone to help."

"I can manage, thanks." She smiled, hopefully diverting him from becoming insistent on helping her. She really didn't want anyone associated with him to see where she lived.

The tiredness in his face smoothed out—his very handsome face, she finally realized, admiring his tall, athletic body.

"Whatever expenses you incur in moving out, I'll pay. Just let me know how much."

"Thank you."

"And if everything works out, I'll buy out your contract from At Your Service. Falcon Motorcars would become your employer, so you'd have benefits."

Benefits. Valerie wished he would leave so that she could sit down. An internal earthquake had her trembling. She was surprised he couldn't see it.

She'd been without health insurance for the year that she hadn't been able to find permanent work. "Feel free to start putting through the new-employee paperwork," she said.

"You're very sure that things are going to work out."

"Three things you'll learn about me, Mr. Falcon. I'm competent, I'm reliable and I'm loyal. I also know I have to prove myself."

"You can call me David." He pulled a large envelope from his briefcase and handed it to her. "You'll find a map to the house inside this envelope, and some general instructions. A few forms you need to fill out. A key to the cottage, in case I'm not there when you arrive." He gestured toward the door. "I'll walk you out."

"I think we both probably have to talk to Denise."

"Right. I'll go first." He shook her hand. "See you later."

"Thank you for the opportunity," she said. *Now go away.* He walked out the door.

She sank into the chair, her knees giving out. He stuck his head back around the corner. "You like dogs?"

"Yes." She tried to stand.

"Don't get up," he said, eyeing her intently. "Are you okay?"

"I'm fine. My foot got caught in the chair leg."

He waited a couple of beats. "Is your daughter good with dogs?"

"She loves them, but she's never had one of her own."

"I have a great old-lady dog. I've had to foster her with my brother and his four kids because I've been gone so much. She looks at me with accusing eyes every time I leave their house without her. I'd like to bring her home."

"By all means."

He slapped the doorjamb and nodded. "Thanks."

"You're welcome."

He disappeared, but she held herself together, in case he surprised her by returning—

"One more thing," he said, again appearing in the doorway. "Can your daughter swim?"

"Yes."

"Good. I have a pool. I don't want to have to worry about her."

"She'll abide by the rules."

"Okay." Then he was off again.

She stared into space. He had no idea what having this job meant to her. None. She didn't care if she had to work 24/7. Didn't care if she lost sleep or weight or her mind. Well, maybe she would care if she lost her mind.

It was a good job, out of the city, working for a man Denise assured her was decent and successful. He'd have to sign a contract, the same as Valerie would, spelling out the details of the business arrangement, including that there would be no sexual contact between employer and employee. She could live with that.

All she wanted was to provide for her daughter.

Finally she could do that.

Chapter Two

"Over there, Mom." Hannah pointed straight ahead. "See the mailbox? That's the address. But where's the house?"

Valerie braked, slowing, then came to a stop next to the mailbox. Ahead she spotted a break in the abundance of trees and shrubs and assumed it was a driveway. She nosed the car down the gravel road, past a small forest of wild oaks, fragrant pines and stately cedars. Then she came upon a wide firebreak clearing and an amazing house, all glass and logs and rocks, reaching toward the sky, the stark edges softened by clouds, the windows reflecting treetops.

"Awesome," Hannah said reverently. "We're gonna live *here?*"

Valerie was no less awed. She'd expected a nice house, but not one that should be profiled in *Architectural Digest*. "Remember we won't be living in the house but in a cottage on the property."

No one came out of the house to greet or question them,

so Valerie continued on, following a gently curving path around the house, discovering several buildings—a four-car garage, what looked to be a stable and the building referred to as the cottage.

The word *cottage* had conjured up visions in Valerie's mind of rosebushes and wood shingles. Instead the structure was a smaller version of the main house, except with cedar-plank siding instead of logs, but with the same large windows, and more space than she and Hannah had ever lived in.

"There's the pool!" Hannah exclaimed, scrambling to unbuckle her seat belt and flinging the car door open. "And a hot tub. Mom, it's got a hot tub. We get to use it, too, right?"

She was out of the car and running toward a free-form pool that seemed carved out of the landscape, with a small, rock waterfall at one end that spilled into both the pool and hot tub.

Gravel crunched under Valerie's feet as she followed Hannah, reaching a flagstone path that branched into others heading toward the cottage, the main house, and through a wild, obviously untended garden to the pool. Lack of interest in gardening, she wondered, or his intent? He must be able to afford a gardener.

Valerie reached her daughter, who'd crouched beside the pool, dipped her hand into it then flicked a few refreshing drops at Valerie. "Can we go swimming, Mom? I'm sooo hot."

They'd spent the afternoon packing their belongings and cleaning their apartment in the 101-degree Sacramento weather, squeezing everything into their small car. They both needed a cool swim before unpacking and settling in. And the man of the house didn't appear to be home.

"Pleeease," Hannah begged, tugging on Valerie's hand.

"How fast can you find your bathing suit?"

"I put it in the last grocery bag we loaded." She grinned, obviously pleased at her planning ahead. "Yours, too. I swiped it from your suitcase as soon as you said there was a pool."

"Have I told you lately how smart you are?" Valerie hooked an arm around her daughter as they returned to the car.

"Just every day."

They grabbed the bag from the car then headed to the cottage to change. A note was taped to the front door: "Welcome. I expect to be home by 7:30. I'll bring dinner. We'll meet later to discuss your specific duties. DF"

It was only six o'clock, so they had plenty of time, provided she could drag Hannah out of the pool at some point.

"Way cool!" Hannah declared as they stepped inside the cottage.

Valerie wondered why David called it a cottage when it was really more of a guesthouse. A large great room, dining area and kitchen comprised the visible living space, while in the back were two bedrooms with a shared bath between. The modern furnishings looked brand-new and perfectly suited to the structure, not exactly "cabin" decor but dark greens, reds and browns, with some wrought-iron pieces and trim, and a stone fireplace.

She'd never lived in anything like it.

"Which bedroom do you want?" she asked her daughter, her words trailing off as Hannah raced into one of the rooms and slammed the door shut.

"Hurry, Mom," she shouted through the wood.

Valerie took a moment to enjoy the bedroom that would now be hers. The pine furnishings included a rustic four-poster, queen-size bed and an armoire that housed a television, drop-leaf desk and six-drawer dresser. The comforter was red-and-green striped. Overall, it was a streamlined, masculine look, but that didn't really surprise her. David Falcon was all male.

"I'm ready!"

"Almost done," Valerie called out as she peeled off her sweaty, sticky clothes and tugged on her bathing suit, a black one-piece as old as Hannah. Valerie found a linen closet inside the bathroom and grabbed two pool towels. On her way out she caught sight of herself in the mirror. Her suit sagged a little, as much from old elastic as the fact she'd lost weight in the past year, leaving her, according to her mother, skin and bones. She didn't think she looked *that* bad, but maybe the new situation—especially the lack of worrying about life in general—would bring back her lost curves, or at least what there'd been of them to begin with.

She would be happy here. She could feel it. She and Hannah would have a place they could call home. They wouldn't have to triple-lock their door. They could sleep with windows open.

"Mo-om!"

Valerie hurried out of the bathroom, grabbed Hannah's hand and ran to the pool, jumping straight in. They touched bottom then shoved themselves up through the bubbles, still holding hands, laughing as they broke the surface.

This is what freedom feels like—cool and clean....

She ignored the hot tears pressing at her eyes. She wouldn't do anything to mess up this incredible situation, would make sure that Hannah understood what her boundaries were. Valerie would make herself completely indispensable to Mr. David Falcon. He would find no fault with her work or behavior. She would be a consummate professional, do nothing remotely improper....

For the next half hour she and Hannah played and romped and floated. They turned on the jets in the hot tub and climbed in, just because they could, letting the heat seep into their bodies, then getting out and doing cannonballs into the cooler pool. Valerie planted her hands on the pool edge to push herself out as Hannah grabbed her ankles, trying to tug her back in. They were laughing and taunting each other.

The stretched-out straps of Valerie's bathing suit slipped a little. She pulled free of her daughter's grip. Breathless, she shoved herself up and almost out of the pool...and came face-to-face with a huge golden retriever—and her boss standing right behind.

* * *

So. The buttoned-up Valerie Sinclair did have a body—a very nice body—beneath all that fabric, David thought, studiously avoiding watching her directly as she jammed her straps back into place and hurried over to a chair to grab a towel, covering herself, apologizing the whole time.

"Hi, I'm David Falcon," he said to the worried-looking little girl clinging to the side of the pool.

"I'm Hannah. What's your dog's name?"

"This is Belle." Belle looked up at him at hearing her name, her tongue hanging out the side of her mouth in a goofy dog smile. She'd become like a puppy again since he'd loaded her in his car. "She'll swim with you, if you want."

"Really?"

"She won't go in on her own, but if you slap the water and call her name, she'll dive right in. Don't call her near you, because she's strong and her claws can hurt. Just let her swim around on her own. She'll climb up the stairs when she's done."

"Cool!" Hannah patted the water. "C'mere, Belle. Come on, girl."

With one last happy look at David she jumped in, thus apparently forgiving him for her years of exile at Noah's. She was too old to be having to put up with all those children, even Noah's sedate children. But having one child around, this eight-year-old Hannah, would be good for her, especially when David was out of town. Belle needed company, and someone to care about, follow around and curl up with.

"I'm sorry," Valerie said again, coming up beside David, watching the dog and the girl swim in circles.

"For what?"

"Not being ready for work when you arrived. I thought we had more time."

"I didn't expect you to work tonight." He finally eyed her directly, all wrapped up in a towel that matched her hazel eyes, her wet hair dripping down her back. He'd been right about her looking younger with her hair down. "Your daughter is a miniature of you."

"I can't tell you how excited she is to be here. The cottage is beautiful."

Belle followed a giggling Hannah across the pool, then headed for the stairs. The dog didn't climb out but stood, resting.

"Are you all settled in?"

"We haven't even unloaded the car yet."

He considered taking a swim himself, but decided to wait until later. He figured Valerie would keep a strict employer/employee relationship with him, which would include making sure her daughter didn't get in his way.

Which was fine with him. David had nothing against kids, he just didn't know how to relate to them, even his nieces and nephews. He particularly didn't want to get attached to an employee's child. She had to be separate from the working relationship as much as possible.

"I picked up a pizza," he said to Valerie. "Come up to the house when you're ready and we'll reheat it. We'll talk business afterward."

"Both of us?"

"Your daughter needs to eat, too, right?"

"I can take her a plate."

"We'll make an exception for tonight."

Valerie nodded. He walked away, sensing her relief. He knew, given her background of false accusations of sexual harassment, that she would be more wary than most, more aware of potential impropriety. He respected that. He wanted a long-term, employer/employee relationship with her. He would be just as careful as she.

He got partway down the path when he heard the thunder of Belle's paws pounding the flagstone behind him, getting closer. He turned. She bounded to a halt and shook the pool water from her fur, head to tail, drenching him.

Hannah shrieked with laughter then clamped a hand over

her mouth. Valerie stood frozen, awaiting his response. He hunkered down and wrapped his arms around his great old dog, getting himself wetter in the process, glad to have her home.

So much for impeccable behavior, Valerie thought with a sigh as she and Hannah walked to the cottage a few minutes later. He'd caught her in her bathing suit, totally goofing off, acting like a kid. How embarrassing. Not an auspicious start to their business relationship at all.

"Belle's a neat dog," Hannah said. "I never knew dogs liked to swim. I mean, I know they can, because there's even a name for it, right? The dog paddle? But I didn't know they would just jump in and swim around."

"Just don't get too attached. She's his dog, not yours."

"But he's gone a lot. You said so. She'll be staying with us, won't she? She can't stay in that big ol' house by herself. She'd be sooo lonely."

Hannah's eyes pleaded with Valerie, who tried not to laugh. Right. *Belle* would be lonely.

Valerie and Hannah unloaded the car, then showered and dressed for their first dinner with the boss. The evening temperature was perfect as they took the path to the house and climbed the back stairs. Through a window Valerie saw a kitchen and was glad she would be working in a space with such a spectacular view, not only of the pool but the tree-studded hills.

She knocked on the kitchen door. After a minute she knocked again. Finally she turned the handle and leaned inside. "Hello?"

"Be right there. Make yourself at home," David called, the words muffled by distance.

"Wow. Our old apartment would fit in here," Hannah said, looking around at the kitchen and breakfast nook.

The stainless steel appliances made it contemporary, but there was a rustic feel, too, in the pine cabinets and autumn-toned granite countertops. Not a curtain in sight, either, nor any plants. Nothing to soften the streamlined feel of the place, the home of someone who didn't really live there, but used it as a base camp.

David breezed into the room. He'd changed from slacks and a dress shirt to jeans and a T-shirt, and was barefoot. Belle trailed him. Valerie wondered how old David was. Thirty?

"Settled in?" he asked.

"Almost. We haven't put everything away, but it's all in the house," Valerie answered, keeping a hand on Hannah's shoulder so that she wouldn't run to Belle, who wagged her tail in greeting.

"The stove's preheated," David said. "Shouldn't take too long. I hope you like pepperoni." He slid a large pizza into the oven. "How about a tour while it heats."

"That would be great."

The inside of the house was as stunning as the outside. It was a man's home, but a classy one, the environment clearly of someone who liked art and color, who had style. Maybe a decorator should get credit, but David would have had to approve everything purchased, so he must've had a hand in the final result in some way.

On the first floor was a living room with a stone fireplace, a family room holding a woodstove that piped heat into the rest of the house, a large dining room with a table and chairs for twelve, an office and a powder room. Upstairs were four bedrooms, two baths and the master suite, with its enormous bed and spectacular view, the same as in the kitchen, of the pool and mountains, even the cottage. Heavy green drapes framed the windows. She wondered how often he shut them.

She wondered, too, how often he had company. Female company. He was an attractive and successful man. Did he have a regular girlfriend?

"It's an incredible home," she said to him, having given

up on keeping Hannah by her side. She and Belle had teamed up, following at their own pace. "Although a lot of house for one person."

"I spend much of my life in airplanes and hotel rooms. I need a place to spread out."

"How long have you lived here?"

"Had it built five years ago."

They headed out the bedroom door and downstairs. Valerie motioned to Hannah, who played on the landing with Belle, tossing the dog's rag doll, then throwing it again after Belle brought it back.

"How much are you gone?" she asked.

"At least half the month. My oldest brother, Noah, and I have owned the business for eleven years. We used to share the overseas work, but Noah's wife died three years ago, and now he has their four children to take care of." They reached the bottom of the staircase, which faced a wall of family photos. He pointed to a photo of a man and woman with four children. "He's needed to be with them, I understand that, so I've been doing all the traveling. But someday I hope we can split the work again. I'm also trying to figure out ways to do less overseas and more here in the States."

Valerie heard frustration in his voice. Or maybe weariness. "How old are the children?"

"He has two sets of twins, as you can see. Ashley and Zoe are twelve. Adam and Zachary are nine. They're…very well behaved."

Valerie wondered why he said that as if it was a bad thing. "You said he was your oldest brother. You have others?"

"One, Gideon." He tapped a photo. "He's the middle child."

"Your parents like biblical names," she said with a smile.

"Our father did."

The man in the picture he pointed to resembled Noah most of all, but she could see David in him, too.

"We have different mothers. This one's mine," he went on

to say, moving to the photo of a young woman, the picture probably taken twenty years ago, given her hairstyle.

"Do you want to eat in the kitchen or on the deck?" he asked in a quick change of subject.

"The deck," Hannah said, focused on the photographs, apparently fascinated. Then she caught Valerie's pointed look. "Please," she added.

"You got it. I'll cut the pizza into slices. There's a salad in the refrigerator. Paper plates and napkins are in the cupboard next to the sink," he said.

They settled around a table on the deck overlooking the backyard. Belle curled up at their feet.

"If you had the house built," Valerie said, "then you also had the stables put in. Do you plan to get a horse?"

"It's a dream. I'm not here enough."

"Do you know how to ride?"

He grinned. "Nope."

"Then why…?"

"Wide-open spaces."

Valerie was beginning to understand him. He needed space but felt hemmed in by his work. He must feel handcuffed or something. And resentful? she wondered.

"What grade are you in?" David asked Hannah.

"Third."

"Do you like school?"

"It's okay."

Valerie sympathized with her daughter. She'd attended three different schools in her short life. It was another reason for making sure she kept her job—she wanted Hannah to have the luxury of staying at one school and making long-term friends. Living a normal childhood, if Valerie could make that happen.

She wondered about David's childhood, if, having differ-ent mothers, he and his brothers were raised together. Maybe they weren't close in age. As an only child, Valerie had desperately wanted siblings, but her father had divorced her mother when Valerie was a toddler and had rarely contacted Valerie since. As far as she knew, he hadn't fathered more children.

When they were done eating, Valerie stacked the paper plates and started to stand.

"I'll take care of that later," David said, then pointed toward the floor under the table. Hannah had joined Belle and was now asleep against the dog, who looked at David but didn't make a move to get up.

"We might as well go over your duties," he said. "I've written them up for you. Be right back."

"What a good dog you are," Valerie said to Belle, petting her. Belle closed her eyes, making a happy sound.

David returned, taking the seat next to instead of across from her. He set a piece of paper on the table between them so they both could read it. She was aware of him, of his arm almost touching hers. He hadn't stepped over any line at any time, either with comments or looks, in fact had gone out of his way not to look at her at the pool until she'd wrapped the towel around her, covering her bathing suit. Not interested? She knew it was better that way, but—

"You're probably worried about working at the house during the night, and leaving Hannah on her own at the cottage," he said. "There's an intercom system between the houses. You'll be able to hear everything that happens in the cottage—or vice versa, if necessary. You just have to set the buttons. There's also an alarm. I've never had problems here, but I know it'll probably make a city girl like you feel more comfortable."

"Okay, good."

He went down his itemized list, explaining each of her duties. He would make his own breakfast but preferred she prepare his dinner. He was rarely home at lunchtime, so they would play that by ear on the occasions he stayed home. Valerie and Hannah could use the pool and patio anytime except when he was entertaining, and then he expected privacy, unless he asked for something.

Privacy for women friends? Valerie wondered. Probably.

"I know how to serve a household," she said. "And Hannah will know to stay in the cottage."

"She's not to work in my house," he said decisively. "I know your mother allowed it, but I think children should enjoy childhood. She's welcome to have friends over when I'm not here, including to use the pool, as long as they're supervised every second."

Valerie's throat closed. She blessed whatever fates had sent her to the At Your Service agency, which had led her here. "That's very generous."

"My childhood was one crisis after another. I don't wish that on any child." He cocked his head. "What about her father?"

"Not in the picture."

A long pause followed. She figured he was waiting for her to expand on her answer, but she had no intention of doing so.

"Okay," he said finally. "I've never had live-in help before, so we'll both be feeling our way through the situation. You should speak up if you think something should be handled differently."

"I will. You'll do the same, right?"

"Of course. I'm sure we'll spend a lot of time communicating, in person and by phone. There's no purpose in holding back. The relationship depends on honesty and openness."

"Like a marriage," she said. Without sex, she reminded herself. Without any physical contact whatsoever. Without innuendo. They couldn't even joke about it.

"I'll take your word on that," he said, flashing a quick grin. "Like a *good* marriage, maybe. But since I've never taken part in that institution, I wouldn't know."

"Neither would I." She let that bit of information set in for a minute without explanation.

He glanced at Belle and Hannah. "And, as you know, I never expected a child to be part of the deal, so we're especially going to have to feel our way through that, figure out what works for all of us."

"Your needs and demands come first. You have to tell me if Hannah is bothering you. She's obviously already made herself at home."

He nodded. "We'll talk more in the morning. You'll have to come to the house for breakfast, since I know you haven't had time to shop for groceries yet. I'll be heading to the office for the day."

He stood, so she did, as well. "Where is that?"

"In Roseville, just north of Sacramento."

"What time do you want breakfast?"

"Eight."

"Okay." Valerie looked out over his property. Garden lights illuminated the pool and pathways, creating a beautiful picture. "Is the yard my responsibility?"

"I have a gardener."

"You do?" She put a hand to her mouth, surprised that she'd blurted that out.

He grinned.

"You like the untamed look, I guess," she said.

"I've pretty much just left it in his hands." He walked to the railing, leaned on his elbows there and looked around. "I guess it's not as nice as it could be."

"It could be a showpiece, if that's what you want."

"Are you saying you want to add gardening to your many duties?"

"Maybe your gardener and I could work together on a new look. Would that be okay?"

"Sure, why not. I'll give him a call and tell him you're the boss."

She'd never been the boss of anyone, unless she counted Hannah. "That would be great, thanks." She knelt down to wake up her daughter, who made sleepy sounds of resistance as she snuggled against Belle. "Bedtime, sweetie."

Hannah finally got her to her feet, although she leaned heavily against Valerie. It had been a long, tiring day for both of them. "Say good-night to Mr. Falcon."

"'Night," she said softly.

"Thank you for everything," Valerie added, still unable to believe her luck.

"It's a month, Valerie," he said.

The grace period. She'd already forgotten about that, she was so sure of her ability to please him.

She nodded. "Good night."

"I hope you both sleep well. Belle, stay," he ordered quietly as the dog started to follow.

Valerie was aware of him watching as she made her way down the stairs and through the yard, holding Hannah's hand and stepping carefully. She didn't look back until they were entering the cottage. She could just make out his silhouette. He hadn't moved.

Her heart swelled at the protectiveness of his actions. She was accustomed to looking out for herself and Hannah, without help from anyone. And although David was her employer, she felt he was also looking out for them.

It was a very nice feeling.

Chapter Three

Valerie had learned to cook at a young age and had begun teaching Hannah when she was a toddler. She wasn't a picky eater. They often read recipes and talked about them—how a dish might taste, what could be served with it. Valerie looked forward to cooking for David, starting this morning.

Hannah was still asleep when Valerie was ready to head to the house. She went into her daughter's room and sat on her bed.

"Good morning," she sing-songed, brushing Hannah's long hair away from her face.

"Mmpff."

"Are you awake? I need to tell you something."

Hannah flopped onto her back and opened her eyes halfway. "I'm awake."

"I'm going up to fix Mr. Falcon's breakfast. As soon as he leaves, we'll eat. In the meantime, you can watch television."

Hannah's eyes opened fully. "I never get to watch TV in the morning."

"Some things are going to be different for us here. We'll have to figure out new rules." She stood. "There's an intercom by the front door. If you need me, push the talk button and shout, okay?" She guessed that's how it worked, anyway. She wasn't worried, since she could see the front door of the cottage from the kitchen window at the big house.

"Okay."

"After breakfast we'll go grocery shopping and stop by the school district office to get you registered, so put on some nice clothes. I put everything away before I went to bed last night. Check your dresser and your closet."

Hannah sat up. "I'm kinda hungry."

"There's a box of cereal and a couple of granola bars in the kitchen cupboard but no milk. I'll probably be gone about half an hour, however long it takes to make breakfast and put it on the table. Unless he has more to tell me or some job to do."

"Mom, I'm eight. I'll be *fine*."

Yes, her grown-up girl. She'd had to mature fast, like so many children of single parents.

When Hannah was settled on the living room sofa, granola bar in hand and the TV turned to cartoons, Valerie opened the door and was greeted by Belle. She got up, wagging her tail.

"Good morning, Miss Belle. I assume you're looking for Hannah."

Belle barked. Hannah jumped off the couch and ran over, falling to her knees and wrapping her arms around the dog. "Belle! Mom, look. Belle came to see me. Can she stay?"

"For now. I'll find out when I get up to the house. Don't let her on the sofa with you, though."

"Okay. C'mon, Belle." They sat on the floor in front of the couch.

Valerie headed out and up the pathway. The morning was exquisite—a crystal-clear sky, the crisp scent of pine in the air, a mild midsixties or so, although probably another hot day ahead.

At the house, the kitchen door was unlocked, and since

Belle was out, Valerie knew David must be up. She'd checked the contents of his refrigerator when she'd gotten the salad out last night, seeing very little beyond condiments, although he did have eggs.

"Good morning," he said, coming into the kitchen. "How'd you sleep?"

"Exceptionally well." He also looked exceptionally good in his khakis and light green polo shirt, a shade lighter than his eyes. His dark hair was still damp. He smelled good, too, fresh from the shower, kind of soap scented or a light, pleasant aftershave. "Could I fix you an omelet?"

"I'll just have cereal, thanks."

"Are you sure? You've got eggs and cheese and—"

"Okay, you talked me into it." He poured himself a cup of coffee from a carafe on the counter. "I made a full pot, if you're interested. Didn't know whether or not you drink it."

It was something she'd given up because she couldn't afford it. "Yes, thanks. Do you have likes and dislikes, foodwise?"

"I like meat and potatoes. And most vegetables. Not a big dessert eater, except apple pie and chocolate-chip cookies. And ice cream." David leaned against the counter, sipping from his cup, watching her whisk eggs and grate cheese. "When you have time today, I'd like you to read through the files I left on my office desk and familiarize yourself with them. We'll talk about them tonight. Tomorrow I'll stay home longer in the morning and show you how to access files on my computer."

"When will you leave town again?"

"Sunday."

This was Wednesday. He figured she should be up to speed by the time he left. They would spend a lot of time together, just the two of them....

She poured the eggs into the pan, moving gracefully and efficiently from task to task, then he saw her realize he was watching her, and her cheeks turned pink. He shoved away from the counter and went to the window, surveying the morning.

"It's so quiet here," she said hesitantly, as if needing to fill the silence. "I feel like I'm on vacation."

"I know what you mean. Some days I can't wait to get home. And now that Belle's home, too, it'll be even better."

"Oh, I forgot! Belle is with Hannah in the cottage. I hope that's okay."

"It's fine. I saw her wander down there this morning and sit in front of your door."

"You'll need to tell me what to feed her, and when."

"Her bowls are in the laundry room, and an extra water bowl on the deck. One scoop of dog food, twice a day."

"When you're gone, should she stay in the cottage with us?"

"If you don't mind."

"I think my daughter would raise quite a ruckus if Belle couldn't be there."

"I figured that." He took another sip of his cooling coffee. He rarely had someone to talk to in the morning, and now he couldn't decide if he liked it or not, accustomed to silence as he was.

"Is this enough food for you or do you prefer a bigger breakfast?" she asked.

"I eat what's put in front of me." Maybe he shouldn't have told her he'd fix his own breakfast most of the time, after all. Maybe it would be nice having her there in the morning, fixing something hot and filling.

"You look like you work out...." Her words drifted.

He turned in time to see her swallow, obviously uncomfortable.

"I mean, you don't look like you overeat." She stopped, closed her eyes. "I mean— Shoot."

He decided to rescue her. "I could say the same about you."

"Good genes," she said in a tone indicating that conversation was over. She tipped the omelet onto the plate next to the toast she'd just buttered.

He came forward, taking the plate from her, not wanting

things to get any more personal—for both their sakes. Maybe he should have let Hannah hang around more, to keep things professional.

"I'll eat in front of the computer while I answer some e-mail, then I'll take off," he said. "See you around six o'clock."

"When would you like dinner?"

"Plan on seven." He went out the kitchen door then retraced his steps. "Don't try to do too much today except get settled and acclimated. I know the house needs cleaning, but it can wait one more day."

"All right."

He didn't believe her. Based on what she'd told him, he guessed she had a stronger work ethic than most. "I hope this works out, Valerie."

"Me, too."

He went to his office and shut the door. His computer was on, but he stood at the window instead, eating, the view of the yard the same as from the kitchen and his bedroom. After a minute he saw Valerie make her way to the cottage, carrying a carton of milk. She didn't seem to be in a hurry, taking a little time to stop and look around, maybe visualizing what she wanted to do with the yard.

He should've probably held off letting her start on any major project until their trial month was up, but what damage could she do in the yard? The worst that could happen was that it got tamed some, thinned out.

Except he didn't want a bunch of flowers planted. He should tell her that before she got started. He liked the natural look, which was why his pool seemed to be carved from the rocks. Women always had different ideas about things like gardens, however. His mother had loved to garden....

An hour later David pulled into the company parking lot in an industrial area of Roseville. The large metal building housed several bays in which cars in various states of completion were being hand built. At the far right of the building were his and Noah's offices. David had been a partner in Falcon Motorcars since he was eighteen, the year his father died, leaving his three sons the business in equal shares. For the first eight years it had been fun, each day a challenge, each job different. But since Noah's wife's death, it had become exhausting.

David tried to hide his resentment from Noah, who was still grieving and had enough on his plate with four children, but the resentment was becoming increasingly difficult to conceal, especially as it was compounded by Noah's inability to see the pressure cooker David lived in daily. If only Gideon hadn't left the company, then the responsibilities would have continued to be more equitable. But Gideon marched to a different drummer, always had, always would. Nothing would lure him back into the family business.

"Morning, Mae," David said to the woman who'd been office manager of the business for thirty years, and Noah's administrative assistant.

"The conquering hero returns." She looked at him over the top of her glasses while continuing to type. She hadn't changed her supershort hairstyle since he'd known her, the color as bright red as it had always been.

"Hero?" he repeated.

"You brought home gold, I hear. Literally."

"Oh, yeah. That."

She smiled. "Nice job."

He'd sold twenty cars to the sultan of Tumari, each personalized, and each vehicle netting a tidy profit for Falcon Motorcars, their biggest single order in their thirty-year history. The sultan required so many gold accessories that they might have to open a mine somewhere. The order would keep them busy for two years, would require hiring and training a few new craftsmen.

"Welcome home," Noah said, coming into his doorway.

He was taller by several inches and heavier by twenty pounds of rock-solid muscle. "I heard you arranged a prison break for Belle."

David grinned. "She's finally speaking to me again." He trailed Noah into his office, both taking a seat on the leather sofa.

"So, you found someone to live in," Noah said.

"Yep. Which is why I took Belle home. Valerie started yesterday."

"If she's good, maybe she'll come work for me when she gets sick of you."

"Don't tell me you're losing another nanny."

"She hasn't quit yet, but she's been there for two months. Shouldn't be too much longer."

Get a clue, David wanted to yell at his brother. His nannies quit for good reasons. "Keep your overly generous job offers away from Valerie," he said instead. "I think she's the one."

Noah raised his brows. "The one?"

"Not *that* kind of one. The perfect employee. The only hitch is that she has an eight-year-old daughter. We're doing a one-month test run." He didn't want to jinx the relationship by talking about it more than that.

"You do seem mellowed out."

"I do?" The idea took him by surprise.

"You're not pacing. Or jingling your keys in your pocket. Like Dad."

David couldn't give credit to Valerie for that, not after less than a day. Maybe the *idea* of how his life could settle down and run more smoothly had relaxed him some, but he couldn't have changed in twelve hours.

"I'd forgotten that about Dad," David said, glancing at the photo of him—with Noah, Gideon and himself—on the wall. "Never could sit still."

The brothers stared at the picture for a few seconds. Dad. Another topic David didn't really want to get into.

Mae leaned into the office. "The third secretary to the sultan is on line one."

David hopped up.

"Third secretary, hmm?" Noah said. "Guess you didn't make as much of an impression as we all thought."

"The sultan's got fifteen secretaries. Having number three call ranks me high," he said over his shoulder as he hurried out the door and into his own office. Fifteen minutes later he slid a note into Noah's line of vision as he talked on the phone: "They added four more to the order."

Noah gave a thumbs-up.

David wandered into the shop. The sound of pneumatic tools created an odd soundtrack to work by, and the journey-men craftsmen stayed focused on the work except to give David a wave or nod.

The bays were filled with four cars in various stages of assembly. At the company's European operation in Hamburg, Germany, eight bays were filled at all times. They had orders for fourteen more cars, plus the twenty-four for the sultan. Most took about two thousand hours to build. The company created three basic models: a two-seater convertible sports car, a larger four-seater luxury passenger car and limos, each custom-fit to the customer's specs, including bulletproofing.

The brothers had increased twenty-fold the business their father had founded. With the new order for the sultan, they'd sealed their financial stability for years to come. David could finally relax a little....

If Noah let him. In that sense Noah was like their father—he could never slow down, never miss out on any potential business. He hadn't taken a vacation in years. But maybe that was because he couldn't handle that much concentrated time with his children.

Which made David wonder about Valerie, and why Hannah's father wasn't in the picture. Had he ever been? Had he abandoned them?

David headed back to his office, channeling his focus else-where, not wanting to be reminded of parental abandonment. It was something he couldn't afford to think about.

Chapter Four

At six-thirty, through the open kitchen windows, Valerie heard a car make its way up the driveway, the tires-on-gravel sound distinctive. Earlier in the day she'd peeked through the garage window and spied two cars: a large mocha-colored pickup and a shiny black SUV. She'd wondered what he'd driven to work, and assumed it was a Falcon car because his other two were American-made brands she knew.

Sure enough, a sleek silver convertible sports car came into view, the sun reflecting off a soaring-falcon hood ornament. One of the garage doors opened and David drove straight in. When he emerged a few seconds later, her pulse thumped in anticipation. Would he approve of everything she'd done? Would he even notice? She'd worked hard all day, never stopping to rest except to sit by the pool for a half hour while Hannah swam, but even then reading the files he'd left on his desk for her.

Her mind reeled with the details of a business completely

foreign to her. Her body ached from scrubbing and vacuuming. But she'd caught herself humming several times during the day. Work had never been so much fun.

Much of her happiness came from the general situation—she and Hannah had a safe, beautiful place to live. She worked for a decent man. And in a month she would have health insurance and a sense of security. All of that would spill over to Hannah, too, who had tuned in to Valerie's stress, especially this past year, even though she'd tried to hide it from her daughter. Worry about ever-increasing debt had robbed Valerie of sleep many nights.

The kitchen door swung open, and David breezed into the room, his hair windblown from driving with the top down. The messy look made him seem younger—or maybe just carefree. At the agency yesterday, his jaw had been as hard as granite, his brows drawn together, forming deep lines that had aged him. By evening, he'd relaxed considerably.

"How was your day?" she asked, locking her hands together.

"Productive." He set his briefcase on the nearest counter, next to the stack of mail she'd brought in earlier. "Yours?"

"The same."

"You get your daughter registered in school?"

"All taken care of. She starts a week from Monday. The bus will pick her up right out front."

He picked up the mail and thumbed through it. "Good."

Valerie stood by silently, wondering what to do. Apparently, she'd been wrong—he'd only seemed looser. He was taut with tension.

"Would you like a drink?" she asked.

"Yeah. I'll get it, though," he said vaguely, perusing the contents of a large envelope. After a minute he looked up at her. "Don't let me keep you."

She smiled. "I'm here to serve."

Everything about him seemed to relax then. He put aside the mail and focused on her. "Something smells great."

"Ribs. They're precooking now, then I'll put them on the grill to finish them up. There's also potato salad, corn on the cob and apple pie."

"Where have you been all my life?"

Looking for you. The wayward thought caught Valerie by surprise. No way was she letting herself wish for something she couldn't have. A smart woman learned from her mistakes.

"I've been out there in the world," she said lightly, "getting enough experience to be a great employee for you."

"I'd ask if you got a chance to look over the files I left for you, but I'm sure you did."

"Yes."

"And went grocery shopping. And made dinner from scratch. And cleaned the house, right?"

"I'm kind of an overachiever."

"No kidding." He smiled. "Where's my dog?"

"Oh! I'm sorry. She's at the cottage with Hannah." She should've thought about that. She should've realized that he would want to see Belle when he got home from work. "I'll go get her."

He put his hand on her arm as she started to pass by him but quickly released her. "Belle can stay put for now, although I'm surprised she didn't hear my car and come running."

Her heart pitter-pattered at the brief contact. She didn't need this. She didn't need this at all. "Belle's probably shut inside. I could use the intercom...."

"Are you nervous about something, Valerie?"

"I gave you my word that you wouldn't know Hannah was here, and the first thing she did was latch on to your dog."

"I believe it was mutual latching. It's fine. Don't worry about it."

Regardless of what he said, she would deal with it as soon as she could. "Do you still want to eat at seven?"

"I think I'll take a swim and kick back for a while. Would an hour ruin dinner?"

"Not at all."

He nodded and walked away, grabbing a bottle of beer from the refrigerator on his way out. She turned down the oven, then headed to the cottage. Hannah was watching a movie, with Belle curled up next to her on the sofa.

"Oops," Hannah said as the dog climbed off the couch without being ordered. They both looked guilty.

"Mr. Falcon is home. Didn't you hear his car pull in?"

"I heard it."

"You need to make sure that Belle is let out so she can greet him. He hasn't seen her much the past few years. He's really missed her."

She looked about to argue but said, "Okay."

"Belle, David's home." Valerie held the door open and hoped the dog understood. Her tail wagged slowly as she passed by, as if apologizing. "You're a good girl," Valerie said. Belle gave a little bark then hurried off, heading straight for the house and her dog door.

"Am I in trouble?" Hannah asked.

"No. You didn't know. Now you do, however." Valerie sat beside her. "I know it's hard on you, not having any friends yet. And I've been so busy all day and ignoring you most of the time."

"It's okay, Mom."

Valerie brushed her daughter's hair away from her face. It wasn't okay. Kids needed friends, and it seemed like every time Hannah made a new friend, she and Valerie moved again and Hannah had to start over. *Please let this work out,* Valerie prayed silently.

She refused to look ahead at the negative possibilities— that David wouldn't be happy with her work or his business shut down or something.

That he might meet someone, get married and not need her anymore.

If that happened, she vowed there and then not to move out of the area. She would find another job and stay put, let

Hannah have a stable life. They'd both earned that. Valerie needed to find some friends herself. She missed having a girl-friend to hang out with.

"When's dinner, Mom?"

"At seven-thirty. Can you make it that long?"

"Can I go swimming until then?"

"No. Mr. Falcon's in the pool."

"Aw, man. I'm *tired* of watching television."

Valerie patted her cheek then stood. "Read a book."

"I'm not *that* tired." She grinned.

"He'll be out of town for a while starting on Sunday. You'll have plenty of time to swim." She moved to the door. "I'll bring our plates here when everything is done."

"We're not eating at the house?"

"Hannah, employees don't eat meals with employers."

"We did last night."

"We hadn't settled in yet, so he invited us. It's different now." Valerie closed the door behind her and headed to the house. She glanced at the pool, saw David swimming laps, methodically, rhythmically, his tempo never altering. She looked away as she rushed by, giving him the privacy he'd given her the day before.

In the kitchen Valerie put on a big pot of water for the corn, then went out to the deck to fire up the gas grill. She set the patio table for one, then realized she couldn't hear him swimming. She looked at the pool in time to see him push himself up and out of the water.

Valerie went still. Water drops glistened off his chest. His swimmer's body was long and lean and perfectly muscled. There was strength there, enough to pick a woman up and carry her, to hold her close....

Belle trotted up to him, waited to be petted. He crouched down and scratched behind her ears, and she wagged her tail, rubbing happily against him. Valerie heard him talk to the dog, but couldn't hear the words.

He stood, toweling his hair, then saw her. She should've returned to the kitchen, pretended she wasn't watching, but she couldn't make her legs work. He was one beautiful male specimen....

He looked away first, then knotted his towel at his hips and headed toward the stairs leading to the kitchen. Her face burned. What would he think? That the sexual harassment claimed by the jerk she used to work for was true? That she'd lied? If they didn't have trust, they had nothing. She was living on his property, would have full access to his home, his computer, the details of his business.

She picked up a grill brush and scrubbed hard at the already clean racks until she knew he'd made his way through the kitchen and she could comfortably return.

Would he say anything? Had she already ruined her future with him?

Her hand shook as she lifted the pot lid to check on the water.

And so the wait for answers began.

David stood under the shower spray, letting the ultramassage setting work magic on his tight shoulders, trying to pound out the image of Valerie watching him. If she weren't his employee, he would be flattered. She was an attractive woman, both soothing and sexy, a rare combination.

But she worked for him, so now what? Just ignore it? Discuss it so they could deal with the situation before it escalated into something uncomfortable, or even impossible?

Man, he needed a date. If all it took was for Valerie to stare at him for a few seconds—

But maybe he was wrong. Maybe she hadn't been looking at him. She'd been a good twenty-five feet away, after all. He could've read something into it that wasn't there. Perhaps his ego had gone into overdrive. His body certainly had, which was why he'd wrapped the towel around himself and headed for his bedroom so fast, before she saw how affected he'd been.

He stepped out of the shower, the question still foremost on his mind. *What should he do?*

The phone rang as he zipped his jeans.

"David? It's Denise Watson. Just checking in to see how Valerie is working out."

Hearing the voice of the director of At Your Service made David's decision for him. He didn't want to interview any more candidates. He wanted his life settled. And maybe he was wrong, anyway.

"She's fitting in very well," he told Denise, grabbing a T-shirt from his dresser drawer. "She's a very hard worker."

"And her daughter?"

"So far, so good." He hoped it continued after Hannah felt comfortable in her new surroundings. You never knew with kids.

"I'm so glad to hear that. You'll let me know if anything comes up, right?"

David almost choked. Like something hadn't already come up when Valerie had stared at him so intently, so directly? "I'll do that."

Belle followed him downstairs a minute later. He could smell the ribs on the barbecue—or the barbecue sauce, anyway. He walked into the kitchen. Valerie didn't acknowledge his presence.

"Smells good," he said.

"Everything's ready." Still she didn't look at him but moved around the room, putting corn and potato salad on three plates then taking an empty platter to the barbecue, returning with a stack of ribs. She piled a mound on one dinner plate. "I set the table on the deck for you," she said, adding ribs to the other two plates. "If you'd rather eat inside, I can move your place setting."

He was a little intrigued now at how she wouldn't look at him. He'd been right. It hadn't been his ego. "Outside is fine, thanks." He took the plate from her. "You don't need to wait hand and foot, Valerie."

"Okay." She slid her hands down her apron.

He wondered where she'd gotten it. He also wondered when the last time was that he'd seen a woman wear an apron at home. It seemed so old-fashioned. Or maybe she thought it put a division between them, a reminder of their employer/employee status.

"I'll be back in a half hour to clean up the kitchen, if that's okay," she said, picking up the two remaining dinner plates and walking away.

"That's fine." What else could he say?

She apparently hadn't thought about the fact she had a plate in each hand, however, because she stopped at the door, looking bewildered.

"Hang on. I'll get it," he said. He grabbed the handle, then waited for her to look at him. Her cheeks took on a pink tinge. "The food looks great. The house is cleaner than it's been in months. I'm not going to make your day longer by discussing the files tonight. I don't need to go into the office tomorrow, so plan on a full morning with me tomorrow."

"Okay."

He opened the door. She slipped past him, the scent of hickory trailing her. He shut the door then grabbed his beer and took his plate outside, Belle following and settling under the table, just as Valerie reached the cottage. She didn't turn around and look back at him.

David turned his attention to the panoramic view, something he never tired of. The sun hadn't quite set but had dipped behind the hill, creating an aura that backlit the scene. Peace washed over him.

After a minute he picked up a rib, the meat so tender it almost fell off the bone. He was used to eating alone at home, although not a meal as good as this one, and he certainly never set the table, place mat, cloth napkin and all. It made him seem even more alone.

He picked up his plate and moved to the railing, leaning a

hip against the wood as he dug into the potato salad. From the cottage came laughter, first Hannah's then Valerie's. Even Belle lifted her head, her ears pricking. Were they reacting to something on television or just making each other laugh? They did that a lot.

He hadn't grown up in a household where laughter was a constant. His mother had left when he was eleven. Before that, his parents had fought all the time, one of the reasons why David refused to fight with anyone. Noah had left for college the same week David's mother left, and Gideon was fourteen and entering high school, so Gideon hadn't had a lot of time for a kid brother. Their father hadn't been an easy man to please.

Hannah laughed again. Did she miss having a father, as he had missed his mother? Hannah seemed well-adjusted enough.

Belle got to her feet and wagged her tail as she looked up at him with soulful eyes.

David sighed. "Okay. You can go see Hannah."

The dog hustled off. Hell, even Belle wouldn't keep him company....

That settled it. Time to take back his life. He would start by accepting invitations, even when he was too jet-lagged. His world had become too routine, too closed in. Too all work and no play.

Time to liven things up.

Chapter Five

"So, your home base in Europe is Hamburg, Germany, but you're rarely there?" Valerie asked the next morning after spending a few hours with David in his office.

He was searching for a particular file on his computer, his focus on the screen. "I go where the potential business is, which means I'm taking a train or plane constantly, following leads. I go to Hamburg only to keep a personal hand in the business, because that's where the cars are built. It's good for the crew to see a boss now and then."

"And you've been the one solely responsible for wrapping up the deals for the past three years?"

He nodded.

No wonder he seemed so tired. It made her want to rub his back....

Valerie picked up her notepad and ran her pen down the notes she'd taken. "When you leave on Sunday, where will you go?"

"London first, then Rome."

She'd never traveled outside of California. It all sounded exotic to her, while to him it was probably just routine, maybe even mundane. "Do you have a favorite place?"

"Yes, a newly discovered one. Tumari."

"Where's that?"

"In Malaysia. It's a sultanate, an extremely rich little country with lots of oil. And it's beautiful. Completely different from the places I usually go." He double-clicked on a folder. "Usually it doesn't matter much to me where I go, since I rarely do anything but work—wining and dining being part of that."

"So you have no interest in vacationing anywhere you've been?"

"Coming home is my vacation. This house is my ultimate five-star resort." His gaze flickered to her. "You have dreams of traveling?"

"I've always wanted to go to Hawaii."

He smiled. "A small dream."

"Not to me."

"I didn't mean you were dreaming small, but that accomplishing it is relatively easy."

She couldn't contradict him without telling him how close she'd been to being homeless two days ago. How long it was going to take her to be debt free. He'd never been poor. "I'm saving my pennies. Maybe for Hannah's high school graduation."

He seemed about to say something, then looked at his monitor instead. "Here's the breakdown of clients, real and potential. How are you with spreadsheets?"

"Classroom taught, but no work experience."

"The data is here in various forms. What I need is for you to extract the data and import it into separate spreadsheets." He opened a blank spreadsheet and showed her how to transfer the numbers, as she took notes.

"What's your goal?" she asked.

"I want to know if there's business potentially big enough anywhere in particular to justify hiring a local rep permanently for the area. I know where we've sold well. I want to know where we've made inroads but no sales success—and, therefore, why. Which models have customers been interested in, then didn't buy? Which engine displacement is being considered? All these things have merit." He met her gaze. "All the information is here, but I need it separated and sorted."

"Okay." Maybe not as hard as it seemed, she hoped. She would need an atlas, though, since she didn't know where a lot of the European cities were in relation to each other. The Internet would help. "Do you want me to work on this now?"

He looked at his watch. "It's almost lunchtime. Why don't you take an hour off and spend it with your daughter. My guess is she's anxious for a swim."

She didn't like that he had to take Hannah into consideration, but she was glad he did. "Can I make a sandwich for you?" she asked.

He stretched. "I'm going for a drive. I'll eat while I'm out. I may take a couple hours."

"Okay."

"Good work today, Valerie. You're a quick learner."

"You're a patient teacher."

"Am I?" he asked.

She nodded. Why did that surprise him?

"I've never been known for patience." He jangled his keys in his pocket for a moment, then pulled them out. "I'll see you later."

"Okay."

He disappeared around the corner then came back into the doorway a moment later. "We never discussed your hours."

"In what way?"

"Obviously you're supposed to have days off. *Need* to have days off. Everyone does. And this job may be sixty hours one week and twenty hours the next."

"Let's not worry about it at this point. I'll keep track for now and see how it averages. At some point I'll probably want a weekend to go visit my mom in Palm Springs."

"Works for me." He left again. This time he stayed gone.

Days off? She smiled as she stood, laying her notepad on the streamlined black and teak desk, aligning the items on his desktop. Her salary was generous already, plus it included room and board. She could work eighty hours a week and it would still be a good deal for her.

Valerie put the computer to sleep, slid David's chair under the desk, then moved hers back into position against a wall. She closed the blinds a little, blocking the sun. After a final glance around the room, she turned off the light and headed for the cottage, but before she reached it, a truck pulled in, a trailer full of gardening tools hitched behind it.

She changed direction and headed for the truck.

A man climbed out of the vehicle, thirtyish, not overly tall, brawny. His dark hair was pulled back into a ponytail and tied with a leather thong. His T-shirt hugged his torso, his jeans were torn in interesting places, his boots well worn. He looked like the kind of bad boy that teenage girls go for before they learn that good men make better partners.

Bad boys—the kind of man Valerie had gone for. Gotten pregnant by. Although he'd been less rough around the edges than this guy.

"You Valerie?" Bad Boy asked, his fingers splayed low on his hips, a knee cocked, challenge in the stance.

She kept her voice pleasant. "Yes."

He angled his head toward the big house. "David says I take my orders from you now."

"What's your name?"

"Joseph McCoy."

She offered her hand. "I'm looking forward to working with you."

His belligerent pose eased a little, but he wore sunglasses, hiding much of his expression. He shook her hand.

"I'll get my notes," she said. "Be right back." She didn't wait for him to respond but headed for the cottage.

"You want to swim?" she asked her daughter as Belle slunk off the couch.

"Yes!"

"Go change. I'll be outside talking to the gardener." She grabbed a notepad from the kitchen counter and left.

Joseph was leaning against his truck, arms crossed. He didn't acknowledge her, even though he couldn't have missed hearing her footsteps. She tapped his arm with her notepad.

"Yeah, boss?" he asked.

Not a promising start. "This is my vision," she said, holding out the notepad for him to take, ignoring his hostility.

He gave her design a cursory look but didn't take the pad from her. "No flowers."

"Why not? Won't they survive the weather here?"

"Most things survive with proper tending. But in this case David specifically said no flowers."

"He didn't tell me that."

"He told *me*."

"I think the garden needs more color variation."

"You can do that with plants. There's lots to choose from. All shades of green. Yellow. Red."

"Why haven't you used them?" She mimicked his hostile pose now, tired of his attitude.

"He never said to."

"*You're* the expert."

"Look, lady, David and I have been friends since second grade. He would've said something if he didn't like what I was doing."

"Mom! Can I get in the pool?"

"Just a second." As Valerie turned back, Belle came running, but straight to Joseph.

"Hey, girl. You're home." He crouched and gave the dog a

good rub. Belle pushed herself against him, knocking him down, making him laugh.

"We need to continue our conversation by the pool so that I can watch my daughter," she said, heading that way, expecting him to follow.

"Yes, ma'am."

She stopped, turned around and looked down at him, speaking quietly so that Hannah couldn't hear her. "Look, I don't know what bee got in your bonnet but don't take it out on me. I'm your partner in this project, not your enemy. I think the place could look spectacular. It's a good basic design. It just needs…refinement."

He seemed to be glaring at her, but how could she tell with his sunglasses in place? Belle looked back and forth between them. He said nothing.

She threw up her hands. "Fine. I'll be your boss, then. Follow me. I'll give you your orders." She climbed the path, gestured to Hannah, who was dancing pirouettes around the pool, that she could dive in, then sat on a lounge chair and waited for Joseph to join her.

He took the chair next to hers. "Bee in my bonnet?" he repeated.

She couldn't gauge if he was making fun of her. "It's just an expression."

"One that grandmothers use." Before she could say anything, he held up his hands. "Truce."

"Why should I agree?"

"I was taking out my bad mood on you. I apologize."

She eyed him for a few seconds, then shrugged. "Okay."

"Thanks."

"Don't do it again or I'll fire you." She grinned.

He gave her a slight salute and reached for her notes and preliminary drawing.

"Were you mad because David put me in charge or because I was critical of how the property looked?" she asked.

"Wow. You're direct."

"Saves time and energy."

Hannah called Belle into the water. Her daughter's laughter was contagious.

"Dixie—my girlfriend—walked out on me this morning."

Valerie angled her head toward him. She wasn't surprised he confided in her, as many people did. She didn't know what it was about her, but even strangers, like this Joseph, poured out their hearts to her.

"Then two of my employees didn't show up for work. Then David called and said I needed to fix the yard, and I should do whatever you said."

Valerie chose the issue that probably bothered him the most. "I'm sorry about your girlfriend."

"She'll be back. It's a pattern. Except she was a little more ticked off than usual this morning."

She wanted to direct the conversation away from his problems. "As for doing whatever I say, that's not true, Joseph. I have a vision, but I don't even know if it's doable. We need to work together."

"I got it, okay? *Teamwork.*" Then he pulled a pencil from his back pocket and redesigned her entire plan.

David chose to drive the Falcon so he could feel the wind in his hair. He'd been shut in the office with Valerie too long for comfort.

She'd smelled good, but not flowery. Not like perfume, but soap. Fruity soap.

And woman.

He downshifted hard as he headed into a turn, an image of her burned into his memory. She'd worn a proper outfit of cotton slacks and a blouse, buttoned to the neck, her hair twisted into some kind of knot, a plastic clip holding it in place. Which left her neck exposed, long, slender, that fruity scent drifting… Peaches, maybe?

He took another curve, testing the limits of his car and his skill, jettisoning Valerie from his thoughts. When he pulled into a parking lot a few minutes later, he didn't even question why he'd come. The only question was, how would he be received?

David shoved his fingers through his hair then headed for an office on the first floor of the professional building. Laura Bannister, Attorney at Law, the sign said in gold leaf on the window. Laura, a Miss Universe contestant five years ago, had hung her shingle in her hometown three years ago, and now had this office and one in Sacramento, near the capitol building.

She was beautiful, sexy and smart. She'd been perfect for him because her biological clock hadn't begun to tick. Career first, she'd said for the year they'd dated—or tried to date, given how much he was gone. Three months ago she'd sent him a Dear John e-mail, ending the relationship.

He didn't know what he expected of her today, except that he needed to do something about his personal life. He was already too focused on Valerie, the last person in the world he should be attracted to. He needed a diversion of some kind.

David opened the front door and went inside.

"Hey, stranger!" said Laura's assistant, who also happened to be her mother. She got out of her chair and came to give him a hug. Mothers usually liked him.

"How are you, Dolly?" he asked.

"Overpaid and underworked."

He laughed. "You always were the exception to the rule."

"I try. Her assistant in Sacramento's the overworked one." She took her seat again. "I'm assuming you came to see my daughter, not me. She's on the phone. Shouldn't be too much longer, though. How's tricks?"

"Tricky." He sat on the edge of her desk. "Business is good. Better than good, even."

"David."

Laura stood framed in her office doorway, looking every bit the beauty queen, even in her understated skirt and blouse, and with her long blond hair pulled back into a twist. She might think she looked more professional dressed as she was, but in truth it made her look hot. All that fire beneath the prim surface. Fantasy come to life.

She also didn't look happy to see him, as evidenced by the way she folded her arms and didn't come forward to greet him.

"Got a minute?" he asked.

"Not really."

"Oh, give him a break," Dolly said, pulling her purse out of her desk drawer. "I'll go get us some lunch. Talk to the man." She winked at David and left the office, the resulting silence deafening.

Laura sighed. "Come in," she said.

He followed her into her office. On the walls were photos of her reigns as the winner of several pageants, starting at age eight. A glass case held several trophies. Her display at home showcased the flashier crowns and sashes.

He hadn't realized until now how much she'd surrounded herself with her memorabilia, as if everyone needed to be reminded of her success. Or *she* did.

The photo of her in her Miss Universe–supplied bikini caught his eye. He hadn't forgotten what an incredible body she had. But…a vision popped into his head of Valerie in her stretched-out black one-piece, her slender body nicely curved, but her suit as sedate as her personality.

"What do you want, David?"

He eyed her client chair but didn't sit. Revelations were coming at him full force—even the reason for why he'd come to see her. "I didn't like the way things ended between us. I should've at least answered your e-mail."

"Yes, you should have. But it doesn't change anything."

"I know." He didn't want it to, except to get it off his conscience. "I wanted to say thanks for putting up with me for as long as you did. I don't want us to run into each other around town and have it be uncomfortable."

"You waited three months to tell me that?"

"Yeah. Sorry." He saw her relax. The frown left her face. "Thanks."

He nodded, then headed for the door. "See you around." Chapter closed.

"Is this some kind of game, David?"

He faced her as she walked up to him. The woman moved like a cat. He'd forgotten that. She put a hand to his chest lightly, just her fingertips, really. Her perfume saturated his pores.

"Interested in a final farewell get-together?" she asked, her tone and expression leaving no room for doubt about her meaning. "We really didn't get to end things well."

"Do relationships end well?"

"Good point. So?"

He was tempted, more than a little. He covered her hand with his. "I don't think that would be the wisest move."

"Maybe not. But it might scratch a couple of itches. Or are you getting scratched elsewhere?"

He'd forgotten how forward she was, something that had appealed to him in the beginning. But now? Now, subtlety—and the scent of peaches instead of perfume—affected him more.

He kissed her cheek. "Goodbye, Laura."

As he pulled out of the parking lot a minute later he felt a huge load lift from him. *Making amends*. He hadn't known how good that would feel. He'd been juvenile to have ignored her e-mail all those months ago.

Now. How many other items did he have on his regret slate that he could wipe free?

Valerie huddled at David's computer, sorting and resorting information to run different reports from the same data. Hannah had begged to help Joseph in the garden, which gave Valerie worry-free time to work. Valerie found David's project fascinating and time-consuming.

The phone rang, his office line. He'd instructed her to

answer his home phone, but they'd never discussed his work number, so she let it go to the answering machine.

"Hi," a female voice said, low and kind of sexy. "I know you can't be home yet, since you just left. But I wanted to tell you how much your visit meant. It was exactly what I needed. And my invitation stands, David. Anytime. Bye."

Valerie sat frozen, staring at the machine.

Well, really, she thought, what did you expect? That he didn't have a girlfriend? Or two? Or three? A handsome, healthy, wealthy guy like that? She'd fallen victim to his charm herself, without his even trying. Imagine what would happen if he turned on that charm full force?

Valerie shoved herself out of the chair and went to the kitchen. She looked out the window, spotted Hannah tugging on a small bush—where had she gotten those gardening gloves?—until she lost her grip and fell on her bottom, hard. Joseph trudged over, said something, to which Hannah nodded, then he grabbed the bush and yanked it out.

Hannah scrambled to her feet. Joseph flexed an arm, showing off well-defined muscle. Hannah flexed hers, showing none. What their conversation was after that was anyone's guess, but they seemed to be joking around with each other, then Hannah got busy tugging on another plant as Joseph broke up the dirt around its base.

Valerie poured herself a glass of water and stared blindly at the cupboards. She should've poured herself coffee instead, she thought, since she'd just been given her wake-up call. She'd tried to see David only as her boss, but she'd ended up seeing him as her knight in shining armor, rescuing her and Hannah from almost certain peril.

Yes, she'd needed to hear that call from…that woman. To know he had someone in his life to take care of his *needs*. He only needed Valerie to take care of his house and office, nothing more. A wife without sex. A stand-in. She'd known that going in.

She heard David's car and wandered back to the window as he pulled in and stopped beside Joseph's truck. The men shook hands, then stood talking. Hannah waved at them and took off for the cottage, knowing her place.

Valerie would take her cue from Hannah and remember her place now, too.

Chapter Six

"Satisfied?"

Valerie looked out at the garden from the deck above it. Joseph waited for a response to her question.

"Very," she said. "You did an amazing job in, what, nine days? The question is, are *you* satisfied?"

"Yeah."

"And are you willing to say I was right?"

"I don't know that I'd go that far." He grinned when she raised her brows at him. "Yeah, okay. You were right. Not that David will notice any difference when he gets back. When *does* he get back?"

"Tomorrow. How're things with Dixie? Has she come home?"

"She's playing hard to get. But it's Saturday. I know where she'll be tonight."

"Where's that?"

"The Stompin' Grounds. We go every Saturday night to

dance. Except last Saturday. But she wouldn't miss two in a row." He leaned his elbows on the railing, surveying the scene.

Valerie had come to like him a lot as they'd redone the garden. He worked hard, which she admired, and was more creative than she'd given him credit for. He may have been taking the easy route before, not doing more than general upkeep, but now he seemed fully invested in the project.

She wondered how he was going to react when he saw the purple sage she was going to plant as soon as he left.

And then the daffodil bulbs she would put in for spring blooming. Just a small patch, but chock-full for a brilliant, eye-catching area of color. And the herb garden she intended to start in pots on the deck, keeping them handy for cooking. And that arc of lavender below the waterfall.

She wouldn't do much, just add splashes of color here and there, mixing up the look of the garden a little, as the seasons changed. She knew she had to choose deer- and drought-resistant plants, had already talked to the garden expert at the nursery.

Joseph turned his head toward her. "Hey, why don't you come tonight, too?"

"To the Stompin' Grounds? Is it a bar?"

"More than that. It's a place to kick up your heels. You'd like it. You *need* it."

The implication being that she was too dull, she supposed. People often misunderstood her calm exterior for a lack of adventurousness. It was only true because she had a daughter to support and raise. Or so she liked to believe.

"I don't have a babysitter, but thanks."

He slipped his cell phone from his pocket and dialed. "Ma? You busy tonight? Remember Valerie and her little girl? Wanna babysit?"

Faced with the real possibility of having to go out with Joseph, she shook her head at him.

"I'll come get you at eight. Thanks." He turned off the phone and grinned at Valerie.

"Joseph, I can't go with you."

"Can't or don't want to?"

"Both." Yet as she said it, she wondered if it was true. She wanted to get out. Do something. And his mother, Aggie, had been over twice during the week, bringing lunch, then staying on to watch Hannah swim so that Joseph and Valerie could keep working on the garden. Valerie gathered that Aggie had practically raised David through his teen years. But go to a bar? Valerie wasn't sure—

A light went on. "You want to make Dixie jealous," she stated.

"Maybe."

"Aha. Well, my fingernails aren't long enough."

He laughed. "No cat fights. I promise."

"You can't promise that. Your Dixie sounds too unpredictable. I'm a pacifist."

"Pretty please? I guarantee you'll be safe from harm."

Why was she even considering it? It wasn't the kind of thing she did....

He bumped shoulders with her. "You know you want to. There's a wild Valerie inside you that's dying to be let out."

Maybe not a wild Valerie, but a curious one. And one who knew she had to keep her thoughts off David, who would be home tomorrow. She should take advantage of his being gone, shouldn't she?

"Okay," she said finally. "But you can't paw me to get Dixie's attention. I'm not playing that game."

"Deal."

"I assume the dress code is jeans."

"Dress code?" His eyes sparkled.

"Don't make fun of me. I don't have to help you out tonight."

"Does David realize just how cute you are?" he asked with a wink.

Hannah came flying out of the cottage then, wearing her bathing suit, Belle at her heels. "I'm ready!"

"I have to get down to the pool," Valerie said, walking away.

He followed, until they reached the path that split into different directions. "See you about eight-fifteen. Bye, Hannah," he called out, waving.

She waved back. Valerie joined her daughter—and stewed about what was to come.

Joseph's mother, Aggie, reminded Valerie of Mrs. Claus, except her hair was bottle black. She gave Hannah a big hug, tucking her against her in a way that Valerie's mother never had. Hannah not only tolerated it but hugged her back, smiling and shrugging at Valerie at the same time.

"Got me eight children and sixteen grandbabies," Aggie said, shooing Valerie and Joseph out the door. "I know how to have fun with kids. Get along now."

"I left a note on the counter," Valerie began as she was pushed from behind. "There're cookies in—"

"Your girl's eight years old. She can tell me what she's allowed to have and do, and I know Joseph's cell number. Scram."

"I'm dazed," Valerie said to Joseph as he drove away from the house.

"She's competent."

Valerie laughed. "I can tell." She felt relaxed all of a sudden. How long had it been since she'd been out without Hannah? More than a year. Since she was forced to leave her job and the co-workers she'd become friends with.

"Where'd you get those boots?" he asked. "I would've sworn you didn't own any, city slicker."

"I didn't until this afternoon." She'd bought boots, new jeans and a white Western-style shirt. She thought she looked pretty darn good.

Valerie hoped she fit in. The outfit had been a huge splurge. She figured she needed to save every possible penny until she knew that David would keep her beyond the month, but it felt so nice to have something new to wear.

The interior of the Stompin' Grounds didn't surprise her, from the dark decor to the twang of the song playing from the jukebox. If the volume dropped some—well, a lot—when people realized Joseph had brought a new woman, that wasn't a surprise, either. He said they came every Saturday night, like probably most of the crowd. Loyalties would be tested.

Valerie saw heads turn toward a corner table in the back and figured Dixie had to be sitting there, but there were four women at the table, all about the same age.

"Bar okay with you?" Joseph asked over the din, which hadn't returned to its former volume yet.

"Sure." She took a seat.

"What's your pleasure?"

Somehow she didn't think asking for a strawberry margarita was a smart move, not if she wanted to fit in. "Beer, I guess."

Joseph held up two fingers to the bartender, then turned around to face the room, resting his elbows on the bar behind him.

"Which one of the four women in the corner is throwing daggers at me?" she asked.

"Probably all of 'em. But Dixie's wearing the red shirt."

Valerie smiled at the bartender, who set her drink in front her. She reached for it, positioning herself in a way she could sneak a look at Dixie. Valerie swallowed hard. The woman didn't look dainty or helpless, for all that her hair was a mass of blond curls. "I think this was a bad idea," she said to Joseph.

"Why's that?"

"You know that saying about if looks could kill? I'm already a dead woman." She decided not to drink much so that she wouldn't have to use the restroom, wouldn't let herself get into a situation where Dixie and her friends could trap her.

"Just ignore her." He took a long sip, then grabbed her hand. "Let's dance."

After a minute the conversation volume spiked again,

although she noticed that people's interest didn't really fade. Heads turned like at a tennis match, watching the two players. One dance led to another, with barely a break to take a cooling sip. A few people called out to him, but mostly he was left alone. Somehow, she didn't think that was normal. It looked like most people sided with Dixie. Valerie wondered what had caused their rift.

"Are we entered in a marathon that I don't know about?" she asked him, trying to catch her breath. "Last one standing wins, if we don't die first?"

"You gettin' tired, city slicker?"

Valerie stopped in her tracks. She spun away from him, walked over to the bar and sat down.

"Sorry," he said, sitting beside her, lifting his beer. "I'm hurtin'. Guess I hadn't admitted that."

It seemed to be a signal to others that it was safe to take the dance floor, like maybe no shootout at the OK Corral was going to happen. Soon it was crowded, too crowded to see the corner where Dixie sat. "I'd like to go home," Valerie said, leaning close to be heard over the noise. "You can come back here after and beg her to give you another chance. But I want out of your drama."

"But it's early—"

"And who might this be?"

Valerie pulled back fast. She'd never heard Dixie speak, but knew it had to be her.

Valerie stuck out her hand before Joseph could say anything. "Hi, I'm Valerie. I'm just a friend."

Dixie's gaze flickered to Valerie, giving her an icy once-over, then dismissing her by turning back to Joseph, who didn't look the least cowed. For a man who wanted his woman back, he sure didn't have a clue how to go about it.

"Is that right, Joey? She's a *friend?* Like that other friend a couple of years back?"

"We were on a break. You even said—"

"Hey, baby. Sorry I'm late," interrupted a low voice as an arm slid around Valerie's waist, making her jump. Stunned by the sudden appearance of her boss, who wasn't due to come home until the next day, she sat speechless, staring at him.

He stuck out his free hand at Joseph. "Thanks for taking care of my girl. I owe you one."

Joseph shook his hand, pumping it hard.

"Have you two met?" David asked, looking from Valerie to Dixie.

Dixie looked suspicious. "Since when did you starting trusting Joey with a girlfriend of yours, David?"

"Joe's my oldest friend. We have an unwritten code."

"A code?" Dixie drawled.

"And Valerie only has eyes for me, don't you, baby?" David's tone of voice was matter-of-fact and almost adoring, which was at odds with his expression, although only Valerie could see that as he faced her directly.

Well, two could play that game, she decided, fascinated at the lengths David would go to protect his buddy. She put her hands on his face, bringing him a little closer. "Welcome home, *baby*."

He went very still. "Sorry I'm late."

"You're here now. That's all that matters."

"Well, kiss her, you idiot," Dixie said from behind, shoving him almost on top of Valerie. "A girl doesn't like to be kept waiting."

He looked at her mouth—

"But a girl also likes anticipation," Valerie said, dropping her hands to his chest—his very nice chest—and keeping him at bay. "And privacy."

He smiled, slow and sexy. "Then I think we should get ourselves home."

Valerie leaned around him and put out a hand. "As I said, I'm Valerie."

"Dixie."

"So I heard. Joseph's been moping about you all week."

"How would you know that?" Dixie may have been speaking to Valerie, but she was looking at Joseph, her expression melding anger and hurt.

"He's been redesigning David's yard. Even my daughter noticed how sad he was, and she's only eight."

Dixie's gaze collided with David's then. "You're involved with a woman with a kid?"

"Shall we go?" he said to Valerie, who was more than a little curious about what Dixie meant, why she seemed so surprised.

"I'm sorry," Dixie said to Valerie. "Geez. Me and my big mouth."

"It's okay." It wasn't, of course, but at least David would have a good reason to tell people why they'd broken up—*She had a kid, you know*. But if he hated kids, she hadn't picked up on that. He was certainly keeping Hannah at a distance because of the professional relationship—Valerie did the same—but the moments David and Hannah had been in each other's company had been fine. He'd seemed at ease.

Dixie put a hand on each of their shoulders. "Dance with your girl first, David. It's great foreplay." She smiled at Valerie as if apologizing again.

The music was loud and fast. "You game?" he asked.

"Sure. But just one."

"I know." He grinned. "I'm anxious, too."

She just barely stopped herself from rolling her eyes, then swallowed hard as he took her hand and moved onto the dance floor, greeting people, introducing her. Then just as they started to dance, the music changed to something slow.

"I think we're stuck," he said, taking her into his arms.

She tried to hold herself away a little.

"Everyone thinks we're lovers," he said, wrapping his arms around her, drawing her against him.

It was a moment out of time, never to be repeated. Why not just enjoy it, she thought? It was only a dance, after all.

Because you're already getting in too deep, and you, of all people, should know better. Fool me once, shame on you. Fool me twice, shame on me.

She let the cautionary words in her head override her body's response to David's nearness. "Baby?" she said.

He laughed, low. "It just popped out."

"Well, you were a good friend to rescue Joseph like that."

"Joseph? Hell. I was rescuing you, Ms. Sinclair. Joe can fend for himself. Dixie's a force to be reckoned with."

"And you didn't think I could handle her?"

He put his head back and laughed. The feel of his chest moving against hers made her forget her need for caution, especially when their abdomens touched, and then their hips.

"Look over there," he whispered in her ear, making her shiver.

She followed his gaze and saw Joseph and Dixie kissing passionately, a reunion apparently under way.

"No, you wouldn't have been able to handle Dixie. Not if she was in full siege mode," he said, as the song continued. "She wrestled in high school. She lifts weights. They both do. It's something they do together. She could take you with her pinky finger."

"I'm scrappy."

His gaze touched her gently. "I'll bet you are."

"What's the deal with them, anyway?"

"They've been together since they were fourteen. Every once in a while she walks away because he hasn't asked her to marry him. And one day she probably won't come back. Joe's crazy to let her slip through his fingers. There's no other woman for him."

"Do you believe that? That people have soul mates? That there's a special person meant just for each of us?"

"I believe that applies to *them*."

Valerie considered his words. So, he believes for other people, but not for himself? It made her wonder. "Why are you home so early?"

"I was done. Was able to grab an earlier flight. Even got a sleeper seat on the flight, so I'm not as worn-out as usual."

"What are you doing *here?*"

"I saw Joe's truck in the parking lot on my way home. When I got to the house, your lights were out. I assumed you were in bed. Your car was in the garage. I decided to hang with Joe for a while."

"He picked me up. His mom is babysitting."

"I figured that out when I got here and checked out the action, seeing the two of you together at the bar. Same as I figured out why he brought you here. I'm surprised you agreed, though. Doesn't seem like something you would do, make another woman jealous like that."

"I told him he couldn't paw me. I told him I wouldn't play that game. I felt sorry for him. I knew she'd left before, but I didn't realize it was such a regular thing with them or I wouldn't have bothered. Except, it was nice to get out, too. And that's probably what drove me to say yes more than anything."

"You've been lonely?"

It wasn't the words so much as the way he said them that almost brought tears to her eyes. "A little."

"I warned you the place was isolated."

"You don't have to get defensive, David. I wasn't complaining. I love living here. It was more about the opportunity to get out without Hannah, for once. Even good moms need breaks."

The song ended. He seemed reluctant to let her go, so she stepped away, breaking the contact, which, indeed, had been great foreplay. Her body hummed.

David called out to Joseph that he would take Aggie home. They headed to the door, bidding farewell as they went, then they were outside. Few stars were visible in the dark sky because of a full moon. Music drifted. She welcomed the cool night air against her skin.

They made their way to his SUV. He opened the passenger door and she climbed in.

"You look nice, by the way," he said.

"Thanks."

"Seriously. The cowgirl look? It suits you."

"Okay." She finally noticed that he was wearing a similar outfit, except his shirt was dark.

They pulled out onto the highway, not speaking again until they stopped in front of his garage. "Thanks for all your hard work this week," he said. "You've already made a big difference."

She didn't tell him how many extra hours she had spent on the projects he'd given her by phone. She wanted him to believe in her competence while she was feeling her way through a lot of it, especially since his kind of business was nothing she'd encountered before, even working as a temp in various places.

"You're an easy boss," she said, grabbing the door handle. Being confined with him wasn't a good idea, not after the way they'd held each other, and he'd whispered in her ear as they pretended a relationship for Dixie.

"You're the first person to say so."

"Really?"

"Yeah. I think we've got some sort of vibe going. You seem to know what I want before I want it."

"I don't have any other distractions, David. No other employees in the office, no drama. It makes it easy to focus and anticipate. And it's worked out okay, too, that you've needed me late at night while Hannah's asleep." She let go of the door handle and faced him, deciding he wanted to talk, and therefore she should listen. It was only part of being a good employee....

"Are you getting enough sleep?" he asked.

"I'm fine. Are you?"

"My body's permanently confused about day and night."

"Let me know if you'd like me to fix your breakfast." She opened the door then, too wound up to stay with him any longer. Too much about him appealed to her. "I'll send Aggie out. What about Belle?"

"Send her, too. I'll take her along for the ride."

"Okay." She hopped out then after a moment turned back to him. "Thanks for the rescue."

"Glad I came along at the right time."

She didn't want to start thinking he would always be around when she needed him, but the coincidence of his coming home early, combined with the timing of his hiring her when she was desperate, didn't escape her.

"Aggie adores you," she said instead.

"Same here. She became Mom for me after mine left."

They hadn't talked about that before. She didn't know the circumstances, only that his father raised him. "My dad left me, too."

He was quiet for several seconds. "And Hannah's father?"

"A long story."

He nodded, but she didn't know what he meant by it and didn't want to get into it now. "See you in the morning."

"Good night, Valerie."

She gave him a small wave, then headed to the cottage. Aggie refused to take any money but did accept an invitation to dinner as payment.

Valerie changed into her nightgown and went to bed, reliving the evening in her head. She heard David's car return and climbed out of bed, catching a glimpse of him and Belle taking the stairs to the back door. The kitchen light came on then went off soon after. After a few seconds his bedroom light came on. He appeared in the window, a silhouette of stillness until he took off his shirt and tossed it aside. He bent over, she assumed to remove his boots, then he pulled his belt free.

He stepped away from the window then. It wouldn't have mattered, as the dim light only backlit him, not allowing for details from where she stood.

She was just about to go back to bed when she saw him come down the back stairs, a towel wrapped around him. His back to her, he stood beside the pool, tossed aside the towel and dove in. He was naked. And gorgeous. Sculpted. She'd seen a photograph of a statue in Greece of the god Hermes, and David's body matched it—muscular, sleek and tempting.

Her conscience niggled at her, whispering that she should give him privacy and step away from the window. Yet she stayed, waiting, telling herself that no one should swim alone, and someone should be watching, just in case.

But she was waiting for him to climb out, and she wouldn't lie to herself about her attraction, even if she couldn't do anything about it. Didn't dare do anything about it.

After fifteen or twenty minutes of swimming lap after lap, he got out. He stood on the side of the pool, lit by the moon, sluicing off water with his hands. She'd like to do that for him....

He reached for the towel. Her mouth watered. Suddenly he seemed to look right at her. She was pretty sure he couldn't see her watching him, but her heart pounded at the possibility, both from fear of being caught and from hope that he might like the fact she was watching, something so out of character for her, trespassing on his privacy as she was.

He held the towel around his hips and headed back to the house, taking one last look at the cottage when he reached the door.

She slipped into bed and pulled the covers over her head, willing the visions of him away.

Because the last thing she could afford was another obsession that would go nowhere.

Chapter Seven

David wandered onto the deck the next morning and admired his garden. The change was remarkable. Valerie was right. He'd let it become too wild, too overrun. Somehow she'd managed to tame it *and* keep it natural. Obviously she had more vision than he did.

He watched her come out of the cottage and head up the path, the view completely unobstructed now with the foliage trimmed. She wore a sundress—turquoise, sleeveless, the skirt soft and flowing, ending at midcalf. She'd left her hair down, held away from her face with a band the same color as her dress.

In the car the night before he'd been tempted to finger her hair. As they'd danced, he'd inhaled her scent, not peaches like before, but something else. Strawberries?

Danced. For all his determination to keep his distance, he'd not only ended up spending social time with her, but dancing, as well. She'd fit in his arms—and against his body—perfectly. He'd wanted her to lean her head against his shoulder. Crazy idea. Stupid idea. It was a good thing she'd forced some distance between them.

He heard the kitchen door open and shut. A few seconds later she stepped through the open sliding door. He realized he'd felt a little on edge as he'd waited for her.

"Good morning," she said, her hands folded, her expression serene. "How can I help you?"

Loaded question, one he put from his mind. She wouldn't like the answers.

"You rang?" she said into his continued silence.

He'd used the intercom, asked her to come up as soon as she comfortably could. "You didn't have to rush."

"I was up and ready. Do you want breakfast?"

"I already ate." Cold cereal. He didn't know why he didn't just let her fix him something every day, but he hadn't been able to, not since the first morning. "I've decided to throw a party."

She lit up. "Oh, how fun!"

"I haven't given one in a long time. And the yard looks impressive, thanks to you, and should be shown off."

"I can't take all the credit. Or even half of it. Joseph reconfigured my design and did most of the labor. Joint effort, but mostly his."

"It wouldn't have gotten done otherwise, so thank you." He'd brought out a pen and paper for her and left it on the table. "Labor Day, I'm thinking, which means you would only have a week to get ready. If you want to use a caterer, I'd be fine with that."

"Oh, no. I'd like to do it all." She sat, pulled the pad close. "What kind of theme?"

"I have to have a theme? Well, a pool party. And barbecue."

"Adults only? Kids?"

"Both." He took a seat. He liked looking at her. He hadn't seen her really excited about anything, as she generally kept a warm but understated demeanor. "My brother Noah and his children. My brother Gideon and a guest. I don't know who he's dating at the moment. Joe and Dixie. Aggie. Mae, from my office, and her husband."

"Is that it?" Valerie asked when he hesitated.

"No. A few of Joe's brothers and sisters. I may add more when I've had time to think about it."

"Will you bring a date?"

Her tone was casual but pitched a little higher than usual. He recalled the voice mail from Laura, letting him know she was willing to see him again. If he wanted to have a date at his side that day, she would probably say yes.

Then he realized he couldn't do that, even if he wanted to. "That could be tricky, since several people now think you're my girlfriend."

She sat back. "I hadn't considered that. That's…awkward. We should come clean with your friends before rumors start."

He tipped his chair back against the railing and contemplated her. "You don't know much about small towns, do you?"

"Meaning?"

"Meaning, by now everyone who knows me, and some who don't, already have us locked as a couple."

"But it isn't true."

"It appeared to be."

She looked at the table, her expression hidden. When she finally looked up, she appeared more serious than he'd seen before. "You have to fix it."

"How?"

"With the truth. Tell people we're not a couple. That I was putting on a show for Dixie, trying to help them reconcile. I can't have anyone thinking there's more between us, David, *especially* my daughter. In fact, I think you should bring a date yourself. *Need* to bring a date, or else no one's going to believe us."

He knew she was right. "I'll make some calls."

"Thank you." She picked up the pen again and got back to

business so suddenly it caught him off guard. "Do you want to do the barbecuing yourself?"

What had just happened? "Yeah, although Gideon will probably take over. He's the chef in the family. But let's keep it simple. Hot dogs and hamburgers. You can go crazy with the rest, if you want."

"What kind of budget will I have?"

"I don't know. Is a grand okay?"

She coughed. "I think I can pull it together for less than that."

"Whatever. And I was hoping you could organize something for all the kids later in the evening, maybe in the cottage so the adults could enjoy some time without them."

"Sure. Do you know a teenage girl who would like to help out? It'd be hard for me to work both places."

"Give Aggie a call. She probably has some names."

"You didn't mention Noah bringing a date."

"He's not going out yet." He'd been widowed for three years, but to David's knowledge, Noah had never taken a woman out, not even for coffee.

"Will you be calling and inviting people or do you want invitations mailed?"

"I'll call. That way I can get RSVPs at the same time." She hugged the pad to her chest. "This will be so much fun."

"I'm glad you think so." He let his chair settle on four legs again. "I want you to take today off."

She frowned. "Why?"

"Hannah starts school tomorrow. You two should spend the day together. Feel free to use the pool as much as you want."

"Okay, thanks." She stood. "And you'll take care of telling people?"

"I will."

He looked at his watch instead of her as she walked away.

He would talk to Joe and Dixie in person, even if it meant waking up the sleeping tigress.

"The whole day?" Hannah screeched happily. "Just me and you?"

"Yep," Valerie said, smiling.

"And we can do whatever we want?"

"Within reason. And budget. What would you like to do? Do you want to go to the movies?"

"Mom, I've watched sooo many movies. I'm sick of them."

Understandable. "So, what appeals to you?"

"I saw a miniature-golf place when we were out once."

"Okay. Anything else?"

"Can we afford anything else?"

Valerie took her daughter into her arms, resting her chin on Hannah's head. "I'm sorry we had such a bad year, honey. I'm sorry you haven't had any treats in so long. Yes, we can afford lunch before we golf, and an ice cream after."

"But we bought new clothes for school."

Valerie kissed her daughter's head, then held her at arm's length. "You can officially stop worrying about money, okay?" Valerie hoped, anyway. Even making it past the thirty-day trial period didn't mean the job was secure forever. But this time she would have more in savings, just in case—as soon as she paid off her debts. And since she didn't think she could lose her job because of incompetence, she would have a good recommendation to take with her, therefore a better shot at getting a new job faster than the last time.

As long as there were no more evenings like the previous one. She had to stick to a professional relationship with him. Period. He was far too tempting.

"Okay, Mom. No worries."

They headed to Chance City and found the Take a Lode Off Diner, where they ate lunch. Their round of miniature golf after was lively as they goaded each other, challenged each other and shared a carefree afternoon.

At an ice cream parlor, Hannah begged, "Please, Mom? A double scoop. Pretty please? It's a special occasion. Just this once."

Valerie slipped an arm around Hannah's shoulders. "Yes, it is. Two double scoops of bubblegum on sugar cones," Valerie said to the teenage clerk, then to Hannah she added, "We'll have a bubble-blowing contest. Winner... Winner gets what?"

"Um. Winner—"

"Hey, hi," said a woman coming up to them. "Sorry to interrupt. I don't remember your name from last night." She laughed. "You probably don't remember mine, either. How're you doing? I'm Sheryl."

Valerie recognized her as one of Dixie's friends, all of whom must be weightlifters. The four Amazons of Nevada County. Had this one gotten the word yet that Valerie wasn't David's girlfriend? "I'm Valerie. This is my daughter, Hannah."

"Hi. Nice to meet you. That's great that Joseph and Dixie are back together, huh?"

"Yeah, great."

"And everyone was surprised to hear about David and you. We didn't have any idea he was involved with someone."

Hannah looked up at Valerie, who tried to laugh it off. "Oh, that. I don't know why anyone assumed that. I work for him, that's all."

Sheryl frowned. "But Dixie said—"

"Honey, our cones are ready." She put a ten-dollar bill in Hannah's hand and prodded her toward the counter, then turned back to Sheryl. "Truly. He's my boss."

"Sure didn't look like it."

"David was just having some fun with all of you."

"Does Dixie know that?"

"I'm sure she does." Valerie made herself smile. "I hope she forgives him. Boys will be boys."

"Don't I know it! Well, I'm glad that's squared away, but I must say I'm surprised. You two seemed so…close."

Hannah came back and handed Valerie her cone and the change. "Thanks, honey." She swirled her tongue over the cold, creamy dessert. "I'm glad you introduced yourself," she said to Sheryl. "We need to get going, though."

She urged Hannah forward and out the door. "Let's walk up the street and window shop as we eat."

"What did that lady mean, Mom? You and Mr. Falcon didn't go out last night. You went with Joseph."

Valerie hedged only a little. "Joseph and I went as friends. He and his girlfriend had a little argument, and he wanted to—" Make her jealous. How could she tell Hannah that? "He wanted to try to make up with her, and he knew she would be there. Then David saw Joseph's car in the parking lot and stopped in to say hi. We danced one dance together, and people just assumed we were dating."

"That's silly." She scooped out a gumball with her tongue. "He's the boss," she mumbled.

"Exactly. And that's how rumors get started. So, if anyone says anything to you at the party next week, you can tell them that."

"Okay. This gumball is too frozen to bite!"

And just like that the conversation changed, which was a big relief to Valerie. Hannah declared herself the winner of the bubble-blowing contest later and claimed, as the winner, the right to having Valerie make her bed for a month. Valerie negotiated it down to a week.

When they got home, Hannah took off toward the cottage to change into her bathing suit as Valerie followed more slowly.

David called out from the deck. "Did you have fun?"

"I beat her!" Hannah shouted. "At golf and blowing bubbles."

"Good for you."

"We're going swimming now."

"Okay."

"Oh, and Mom told that lady that you weren't on a date with her."

He straightened. "Um. Good."

She rushed into the cottage. The door slammed behind her.

"That lady?" he asked Valerie.

"Sheryl. We ran into her at the ice cream parlor. I hope you were able to clear things up, because I gave her the scoop."

"Was that a pun?" He grinned. "Hold on a sec. I'll come down rather than yell."

Valerie didn't know what to do with her hands. If she crossed her arms, she would look defensive, so instead she picked dead leaves off the nearest bush until he came up beside her. She didn't look at him, just kept scrounging for leaves. "So, everything is squared away?" she asked as Belle bumped her nose against Valerie's leg, looking to be petted.

"I don't know that everyone has heard yet, but the grape-vine has been activated."

She scratched Belle behind her ears, Belle's tail wagging slowly. "What happened with Dixie?"

"She actually found it endearing that Joe tried to make her jealous. Apparently he hasn't done that before."

Valerie closed her eyes, relieved. "We got lucky."

"I didn't say that. She's forgiven *him*. I don't know about us. You in particular."

So much for her first foray into the new town. "And you'll invite a date for the party next week, so there's no doubt in anyone's mind that you and I aren't…a couple?"

"I already did."

So fast? Valerie wasn't prepared for her reaction, as if someone had punched her. "Great." She straightened. Belle wandered off toward the cottage. Standing so close to David reminded Valerie of how it felt to be in his arms, safe and excited at the same time.

He's not your knight, she reminded herself. He's your boss. And you need to keep it that way.

She gestured toward the cottage. "I'd better go change. Hannah will be waiting."

"Have a nice swim." He turned around.

"Did you have a good day?"

"I drove all over town, clearing up misperceptions and extending invitations. I haven't talked to Joe's brothers yet, but everyone else said yes."

"So, your brothers live nearby?"

"They're both in Chance City, but we've got a few miles separating us. You have any siblings?"

"No. I wish I did."

"Yeah. Most of the time they're great. I see Hannah's waiting for you. I'll let you go."

"Mo-om. Why aren't you ready?"

"Give me three minutes." Valerie hurried off. She'd gotten a new bathing suit, still a modest one-piece, but one that fit her well.

He has a date. She pulled off her clothes, stepped into the light blue suit and shimmied it up her body. The woman who'd left a message for him? Probably.

Or maybe not. He could be dating five different women, for all she knew.

Because, really, when it came down to it, she didn't know him at all. She just knew it was getting harder day by day to think of him only as her boss.

Chapter Eight

Valerie scanned the Labor Day party crowd as she set a tray of chips, salsa and guacamole on a table near the pool. No one new had arrived in the past fifteen minutes, while she'd been in the kitchen.

David's date was fashionably late, as were his brother Gideon, and Joseph and Dixie. Valerie counted heads in the pool—nine—eight children, plus one of Joseph's brothers. Two teenagers, Mindy and Jessica, were lifeguarding, then would entertain the kids later in the cottage.

During Hannah's first week in school, she'd made a friend, Gabby, who'd been invited to join the fun. The two eight-year-olds huddled in one corner of the pool, whispering and giggling. Most of the noise came from Joseph's sister's two children, who propelled themselves like seals out of the pool onto the deck, then did cannonballs back into it, screaming, until Mindy and Jessica managed to quiet them a little, probably by bribery. Valerie understood now what David meant—by comparison to the other children in the pool, Noah's kids were well behaved and quiet. Too quiet for nine- and twelve-year-olds.

Valerie headed back toward the house thinking how quickly she'd become used to the peacefulness of David's property, because, in contrast, the party noise seemed as loud as a rock concert, even though the music coming from the outdoor speakers wasn't booming. Conversation was steady and normal, except for Aggie's contagious laugh. Even David's brother Noah was laughing.

An interesting man, Valerie thought, assessing him. He was taller and broader than his youngest brother, and although he didn't pace, she sensed a high level of energy and impatience. He watched his children most of the time, frowning, although whether from concern or disappointment or something else altogether, Valerie didn't know.

She looked for David as she climbed the stairs to the kitchen but didn't see him. Was he worried about his date's late arrival? Annoyed? Angry? Perhaps she had called David on his cell to say she would be late—or not coming, after all.

"The party can start now!" bellowed Joseph as he and Dixie strolled up the driveway, having parked out front.

Valerie was glad to see them holding hands. She'd worried all week about facing Dixie again. Would she turn her back on Valerie for her part in the game last weekend? Valerie wanted to make friends, especially girlfriends, to make a real community for herself, as Hannah was already doing.

But her daughter could also use a strong male role model, something that Valerie had been denied after her father left her and her mom....

And maybe it was the reason for some of her own problems, she was finally coming to realize, perhaps even why she'd ended up in trouble at her last job, not to mention getting pregnant out of wedlock.

Since David couldn't be that role model for Hannah, it was up to Valerie to find someone who could. Having girlfriends could lead to finding a boyfriend. It would force her to get out and mingle, the first step in expanding her social life.

"Coming up or going down?" David asked, startling her, obviously on his way down the stairs, his arms loaded with cartons of soda to add to the depleted supply by the pool.

"Up. To the kitchen. Joseph and Dixie just arrived."

"Couldn't miss hearing that," he said. "It's going well."

"Everyone knows each other, though, right? Makes it easy."

"Easier, anyway. Small towns make for interesting histories."

"Like what?"

"Like Noah and Joe's brother, Jake. He's in the pool with his nephews. Big rivals in high school, not just in sports, but academics and campus politics."

"And girls?"

"That I don't remember. Noah is seven years older than me. We didn't really become close until our dad died and we ended up sharing the business. By then Noah was married and had Ashley and Zoe. I only remember his and Jake's rivalry in high school because I was friends with Joe, so I heard the trash talk at both houses."

"It looks like there's still a feud going on. Jake's playing with all the kids rather than standing and talking to Noah, as his other brother is." She slanted a look at David. "So, if you knew about the rivalry, why'd you invite Jake?"

He hesitated then finally said, "I'm hoping."

"Hoping what? For a fight?"

"Honestly? Yeah. Not a fight, but something to shake Noah up some."

"Look what the cat dragged in!" Dixie announced as a man and woman came up the driveway. "Good grief, Laura. Couldn't you do better than that?"

Dixie was grinning, so Valerie gathered that she and the man knew each other well enough to make a jibe like that. She recognized Gideon from the photographs on David's wall. And "Laura" would be Laura Bannister, David's date.

She was stunning, with her long blond hair, shorts and body-hugging T-shirt. And what a body her clothes hugged.

Valerie felt a swoosh of air as David went past her and down the stairs to greet the new arrivals. Would he kiss her hello?

No. A brief hug, then a handshake with Gideon, who had come without a date.

Valerie hurried on up to the kitchen, from there not once glancing out the window as she finished putting food on platters. She started the gas grill to preheat it, keeping to the timetable she and David had decided on.

After a minute she gave up avoiding looking at him and his date and searched them out. They stood with several people, Laura putting her hand on his arm now and then, smiling at him, her body language announcing how comfortable they were with each other physically.

The pain that stabbed Valerie in her chest didn't catch her completely off guard. During the past week, she'd spent a great deal of time with David as they worked together on projects. With Hannah in school most of the day, the house seemed way too intimate. No one needed her attention. No one dropped by. Valerie and David had almost lived in his office. She made sure they never touched, not even innocently. She'd petted Belle a lot.

But he complimented Valerie on her abilities and teased her a little when she got too serious, and she'd enjoyed being with him.

Which made it hard to see him with that woman, Laura, who looked like every man's fantasy.

The kitchen door opened and Dixie breezed in. A headband kept her tight blond curls away from her face, taming them slightly. But nothing about her well-defined muscles seemed tame.

She crossed her arms and tapped her foot. "Well, if it isn't David's...girl? Isn't that what he called you? His *girl?*"

"He explained the situation to you, right?" Valerie asked, almost holding her breath. She didn't like conflict, and this could easily become one.

"I don't like liars," Dixie stated.

"Neither do I." Valerie stood up straighter. "I did your boyfriend a favor so that you two could make up. Am I sorry I did it? Yes. I didn't understand how small towns operate. I wanted to make friends here, and now everyone thinks I'm not a good person. If I had it to do over, I wouldn't agree to go to the Stompin' Grounds."

"Is that an apology?" Dixie asked after giving Valerie a piercing look.

"Yes." *Please don't make me get on my knees.* She'd promised herself after she got pregnant with Hannah and all that followed that she wouldn't ever beg anyone again.

"Yeah, okay," Dixie said finally. "I actually thought it was kinda cute of Joseph to plan something like that. Anything I can do to help?"

Situation defused, just like that. "No, but thanks."

"Do you want me to round David up for you?"

"I hate to take him away from his date." She wished she had something left to do, to keep her mind off the woman.

"Boy, that's a shocker, isn't it? I mean, I thought they'd split up months ago." Dixie grabbed a carrot stick and took a bite. "I had no idea they'd started up again."

It was her own fault, Valerie thought. She'd made him bring a date so that everyone would know there was nothing between David and her except an employer/employee relationship.

"Well, I have no problem telling David you're ready for him." She opened the door, then stopped. "Would you like to get together for lunch or something sometime?"

"I'd love to, thanks."

"We'll figure out a time and place before the party's over."

"Great."

"You want me to invite Miss Universe so you can get to know her better?"

Valerie smiled at the nickname, which suited Laura Bannister to a T. "Do you call her that to her face?"

"Well, no, since it would remind her she was only first runner-up. I'm not *that* catty." She grinned and left.

Valerie stared at the platters of food. Laura was the first runner-up to Miss Universe? Seriously? Which meant she'd been Miss USA. Miss California. Miss…whatever else.

How was she supposed to compete with—

Valerie squeezed her eyes shut. She wasn't competing, couldn't compete. Which made this the best news possible, because now she knew he wouldn't be tempted by her, either, not with Miss Universe in the picture.

She should be relieved.…

"So? You and Laura again?" Gideon asked, seated on a lounge next to David, both of them watching the woman in question play pool volleyball, her bikini-clad body a sight to behold, perfection in motion.

David glanced at his middle brother and shrugged. "I'm not sure yet."

"She seems to be into it, if I'm any judge of such things. But you seem to be holding her at bay."

One of Gideon's strengths was his above-average understanding of human nature. It had made him a good pitchman for Falcon Motorcars, for gauging the right kind of sales pitch for the individual. Unfortunately, his business sense wasn't always as accurate as his people sense. "I don't want to make the same mistake as before," David said.

"Of?"

"Of starting a relationship that requires too much patience and understanding of a woman."

"Very wise."

"Yeah." David swigged his beer. "Not personally satisfying, however."

Gideon flashed a grin. "Not getting any, huh?"

"Nope." Although Laura's offer had been made and was waiting to be accepted.

"That new housekeeper of yours is a looker," Gideon commented.

"No trespassing, bro. She's the best thing that's happened to me in years."

Gideon raised his hands in surrender. "I won't poach."

"Damn straight you won't." He followed Valerie with his gaze as she cleared tables. She hadn't mingled much, although he had encouraged her to. She and Dixie and Joseph had talked a little, and Aggie was never to be ignored, but otherwise, Valerie had worked, quietly, efficiently, occasionally giving Hannah a hug, whispering in her ear, getting a nod or giggle in return.

David caught Valerie eyeing Laura, who'd scored a point in the pool and was whooping about it. Competitive, sexy Laura. David wondered what Valerie thought of her. As far as he could tell, they hadn't exchanged words.

Noah joined his brothers. It was rare for all three of them to hang out together anymore, given David's overseas schedule, the demands of Noah's home life and Gideon's ongoing projects, which took him far afield at times. Belle wandered over and curled up at David's feet.

"She's ignored me all day," Noah said, angling his head toward the dog.

"You're a bad dream she's trying to forget." David grinned.

"She had it pretty easy. Lots at my house to keep her active." He grabbed a slice of watermelon from the tray beside him and took a bite. "So, what've you got your hands in these days, Gid?"

"A project near Tahoe. In fact, I've been meaning to talk to you both. See if you want in on the ground floor."

David exchanged a look with Noah. Gideon had sold his share of the business to them years ago, not wanting any part of the family business. Since then nothing had turned to gold for him. Although he'd managed to keep out of bankruptcy, just barely, he'd lost his wife because of the risks he'd taken. She'd walked out two years ago.

"We came to an agreement about you asking for money," Noah said quietly. "You want our input on your business plan, we're there for you. But our money's tied up in Falcon and needs to stay there, where it's safe."

"I hear business is booming. Something about a sultan and a whole lot of orders."

"Which means more in expenses, too. Employees, manufacturing, work space. You know that."

"Don't say I didn't give you a chance," he said lightly, but David sensed a bit of desperation.

"Do you need a loan?" he asked. "For yourself, personally, I mean?"

Gideon's jaw hardened. "I'm fine."

"You could come back to Falcon." David didn't look at Noah when he made the offer, but he felt the breeze die and the air heat up from Noah's direction.

"Not interested, thanks."

"Remember, he doesn't look back," Noah said, sarcasm heavy in his tone. "Forward. Only forward."

"What's wrong with that?" Gideon asked. "Wallowing in the past may feel good, but it doesn't get you anywhere."

Noah straightened. "I don't wallow."

"The hell you don't. You wear your grief like a suit of armor. That's what keeps you upright, instead of standing on your own two feet."

"What do you know about grief?"

"Nothing about having a wife die, I admit, but I do know David's wiped out. Look at him, Noah. Just look at him. He's aged ten years in three."

Noah fired a look at David, who didn't know what to say. He hadn't talked to Gideon about the situation, but he couldn't deny Gid's words. He hoped Noah understood his silence was agreement.

"David knows what's important. He does what needs to be done. He's a company man. I've got enough leads to keep David in Europe for a month. And he'll go do the job without complaint. If you cared enough about him, you'd come back and help out for a while. It'd give you money in your pocket, anyway."

"Been there, done that, don't wear the T-shirt anymore."

Noah stood. "I don't need this crap." He walked away, his stride long and heavy.

"Why don't you speak up for yourself?" Gideon asked David.

David was trying to absorb the bombshell that he would be expected to stay overseas for a month. "He has four kids who need him. He can't go running off to Europe every month the way he used to."

"Martyr."

"He's not—"

"You, bro. You. You lost Laura over it once. Probably will again."

"If the relationship had been right, it would've stuck." His gaze found Laura's. She smiled, more than a little flirtatiously. Why was she doing that? Why was she interested? Nothing had changed. Nothing *could* change, except to get worse.

"You'll never get married with that attitude," Gideon said.

"Why would I want to do that? As far as I'm concerned, the only reason to get married is to have children. I have no interest in being a father. Like you, Gid, I've witnessed too much marital misery to fall into that trap."

"The difference is, I still believe in it."

"Even though Jeanne left you?"

"Should I serve dessert now?" Valerie asked from behind him. Her calm voice washed over him. He was grateful for the interruption, would figure out the mess with Noah later. It was party time now. "Why don't you just sit down for a few minutes and get to know my brother, Valerie. Everyone is fine for now."

She hesitated. He knew that she felt her place today was as his party giver, not partygoer. He hadn't seen her sit all day, not even to eat.

Laura climbed out of the pool, pushing herself up and over the edge instead of climbing up the stairs, giving him an eyeful of cleavage. Even Gideon stared, his beer a couple of inches from his mouth.

Laura flicked her dripping fingers at David. "Why don't you come in for a while. It's heavenly." She came up to him, her slick, taut body so close he could've licked the water drops off her.

But he didn't want to, he realized. Well, that wasn't entirely true. What he didn't want was the complication that would follow. He'd been wrong to invite her today, had invited her only to protect Valerie's reputation, and now he was paying for it.

He looked to where Valerie had been standing, saw she was gone. The woman moved as quietly as a butterfly.

He spied her talking with Aggie, who leaned close and said something that made Valerie laugh so much she bent over, her hand pressed to her chest.

He'd very much like to know what made her laugh like that.

Aggie and Dixie made a grand entrance into the kitchen at the end of the evening as Valerie was packaging leftovers. They didn't ask if she wanted help but just pitched in, the conversation light and fun. Dishes were washed and put away, and the kitchen tidied in what seemed like five minutes.

Valerie would never have asked for help, and even found it hard to graciously accept it, but she did, relaxing then enjoying their company. Both women hugged her before they left.

David was huddled with his brother Gideon in chairs by the pool as she passed by, headed to the cottage. She tossed a wave in their direction.

"It was a great party," David called out. "Thanks."

"My pleasure."

Hannah was already in bed. Valerie tiptoed in and found her sound asleep. She brushed her daughter's hair away from her face, kissed her cheek, then headed to the shower.

As she stood under the spray she thought about the day, how much fun it had been to plan the party and fix the food. She'd enjoyed being part of the group, but was also glad to have her job to do, giving her reasons to disappear for a while and regroup. Not that people hadn't welcomed her or had made her uncomfortable in some way, but seeing David with Laura had bothered her more than she'd expected it would. Not only because Laura was beautiful and sexy, but because she *was*. She existed.

Hannah had seen them talking by the side of the house, then hugging goodbye a little while ago. She was a big part of David's life.

"Which is good," she said aloud. "Necessary." She was sure it would help keep her attraction in check. Well, mostly sure. It was hard to control what didn't want to be controlled.

Valerie got out of the shower and dried off. She moved into her dark bedroom and stood at the window. David was alone. He'd settled in a lounge chair, tucked his hands behind his head, looking toward the sky. Or maybe his eyes were closed. She couldn't tell from where she stood.

She dropped her towel and reached for her nightgown, then left it sitting on her bed as she stood, silent and still, watching the man who was fast becoming way too important to her. And way too exciting. Her body felt heavy and achy. Needy.

Finally he stood, walked to where the light switches were, then turned off the lights, leaving only what light a partial moon provided. She could barely make out him peeling his shirt overhead and tossing it on the lounge, then his shorts. He scratched his belly, stretched, then dove into the pool.

She wished she could join him, wished she could see him

up close, admire the perfect details of his body. In the short time she'd been with him, she'd put on a few welcomed pounds, and she felt much more womanly, more desirable. She wanted him to notice; she didn't want him to notice.

She was one mixed-up woman, she decided, forcing herself to put on her nightgown and get into bed before he climbed out of the pool.

Who would have ever thought she would turn into a voyeur?

Chapter Nine

Valerie grabbed the hose and began to wash down the pool deck the next morning after Hannah boarded the school bus. She loved this time of day, was grateful she didn't have a normal nine-to-five routine. Maybe she worked more hours than the average office worker, but she had no commute, no office wardrobe to purchase, no time clock to punch. The trade-off worked for her.

She turned the hose nozzle to jet and attacked some stubborn debris trapped in a corner. David was leaving again today. This time he didn't have a return date.

The image of him with Laura yesterday still clung tenaciously to Valerie's memory. Every man had watched her climb out of the pool, her bikini leaving plenty of skin and curves to admire. Then there was the hug Valerie had seen between Laura and David at the end of the evening.

Valerie had avoided Laura all day. Aside from a greeting at their introduction and a good-night later, they'd said nothing to each other, Valerie staying out of her range.

Then there was the moment when Valerie had accidentally overheard David and his brother Gideon talking. David had called marriage a trap, one he wasn't going to fall into. Where did that leave Laura? Did she know how he felt? Why was he so opposed to marriage?

Something touched her shoulder. She jerked around, hose in hand, avoiding spraying David only because he grabbed the nozzle, diverting the stream.

"Oh, I'm so sorry," she said, turning it off, stopping the flow.

"That's my line. I didn't mean to scare you."

What scared her was how much she wanted to put her arms around him and kiss him. She didn't want him to leave… but she needed him to.

"Guess you were off in another dimension," he said.

"I was just thinking how much I love my job. How diverse it is, and how flexible."

"Speaking of which, I just got off the phone with Denise Watson. I asked her to send me a statement to buy out your contract from At Your Service. Mae Carruthers—you met her yesterday, the company linchpin?"

She nodded, words escaping her. He wanted her. Before the thirty-day test run was done…

"Mae will send you the new-hire paperwork to fill out and return. It can't be finalized until I get back from this trip, whenever that is, but as far as I'm concerned, you're hired permanently."

"Thank you," she managed to say.

"Valerie, I have never worked with anyone like you. You seem to know what I want before *I* know what I want. Everything you touch turns to gold."

"Don't put me on a pedestal, David. I'm not perfect."

"Well, you're perfect for me. I take it you're in agreement?"

She was perfect for him—as his employee. "Agreement?"

"On the job? You want to stay on, right?"

Only more than breathing. "Yes."

For a second it looked as if he was going to hug her. She made eye contact. Waited.

Then he took a step back abruptly, firmly. "I'll call you when I get to Hamburg."

Just her imagination, then. He seemed fine. Normal. "Okay," she said. "Have a good flight."

"I don't know one from another anymore." He left.

She watched him grab his suitcase and briefcase from the bottom step and head to the garage. She went toward to the building, too, not wanting him to go. Crazy. You're crazy, she admonished herself. There were too many reasons why she couldn't let herself feel that way about him.

He backed the car out, saw her and stopped. The passenger window lowered. She walked over to it, leaned down.

"Did you need something?" he asked.

Before she could answer she saw his gaze dip down to where her blouse was gaping, giving him an eyeful. Stand up, she ordered herself. Maintain your professional relationship. But she didn't move. He didn't let his gaze linger, but lifted it to reconnect with hers.

His hand clenched the steering wheel. "You want something?" His voice was tight.

"I was just going to wave goodbye."

He lifted a hand, then backed up, made a quick turn and he was off. Gone.

She wandered back to the deck and picked up the hose. Was he...attracted? Or was it just her imagination—or wishful thinking? No, not wishful thinking. She couldn't wish that way at all.

She opened the hose nozzle full force. A few seconds later a car pulled in. She didn't recognize the bright red Miata, but she headed to the driveway. Laura Bannister climbed out of the car.

A chunk of hot lead landed in Valerie's stomach. How could she have forgotten about the woman? David's girlfriend.

"Hi," Laura said breezily, shoving her sunglasses up. She

looked chic and graceful in her silk blouse, short blue skirt and three-inch heels "Valerie, right?"

"Yes, Ms. Bannister. I'm sorry. You just missed David. He's on his way to the airport."

"Actually, I came to see you."

Valerie kept her expression impassive, but curiosity ran a marathon inside her. "How may I help you?"

"I was hoping you would share your recipe for the potato salad yesterday. I heard you did all the food yourself." She smiled engagingly.

Valerie could see why she'd won beauty contests. Valerie needed to try to like the woman, since they would probably see each other frequently. It wasn't wise to alienate the boss's girlfriend. "I'd be happy to share the recipe. Come on up."

Valerie let Laura lead the way, grateful the kitchen was spotless after last night. It was what she did well. Even if Dixie and Aggie hadn't helped, Valerie would've had it cleaned up before she'd gone to bed.

Most of her cookbooks were in the cottage, but the recipes she'd used for the party she'd left in a drawer. She grabbed the one Laura wanted.

"Um. I'll make a copy for you." She headed toward David's office.

"You're a life saver," Laura said. "I can stop by the market during my lunch hour."

Valerie stopped. "You're making this for tonight?"

"Yes. Is there something wrong with that?"

"It's just that it takes a while. You have to cook the potatoes and cool them. Chop up everything. Mix it with the dressing. Let it sit so that the flavors marry."

"Oh. Well, maybe I'll just buy some this time. But I'd still like to have the recipe."

What was going on? Valerie wondered as she made a photocopy. She didn't know Laura well, but she seemed nervous, and Valerie had figured she was usually well controlled. A woman didn't win beauty pageants without a lot of poise. Lawyers weren't slackers in that department, either. Something else was happening. Laura Bannister was here for a different purpose altogether. Her arriving just a few minutes after David left seemed odd, too.

"Here you go," she said, handing the recipe to Laura. "I've got some salad left over, though, and I'd be happy to share. How many people are you serving?"

"Oh, you're a doll! Thank you so much. Is there enough for four?"

"I think so." She grabbed a plastic container from a cupboard and got out the salad, then decided to just give Laura the whole thing. It wasn't Hannah's favorite food, anyway. She wouldn't miss it.

After more thanks, Laura headed to the door then stopped there. "I forget how long David is supposed to be gone this time."

Really? If it were *her* boyfriend, Valerie would have all the details of his itinerary. "He didn't know for sure."

"Oh, that's right. He told me that. Well, thanks again."

She went out the door in a hurry, almost slamming it. Valerie followed more slowly. She finished hosing down the deck, all the while trying to sort out what Laura had been up to. A fishing expedition for information, at least, she decided. But why? And she doubted very much that Laura cooked a lot, or she would have known that potato salad wasn't a quick dish to make, at least not the traditional kind that Valerie had made.

So, it was personal.

Her cell phone rang. She saw it was her mother. Taking a steadying breath, she sat in a lounge chair. "Hi, Mom."

"Hey, stranger."

Guilt. Just what she needed. She loved her mom, but… "I know. I'm sorry. I've been settling into a new job and home, and I didn't want to jinx things by telling you too soon."

"Keeping your mother informed is jinxing?"

Valerie refrained from noting that her mother hadn't called

her, either. "I've got a great job, Mom. The best I've ever had. But it was a trial run first, and now I've been hired full-time." She told her mom about David and the job.

"You always were able to land on your feet."

Valerie took the blow in silence, and rethought her idea about going down for a visit. Except that she wanted Hannah to know her grandmother.

"I've worked hard, Mom."

"Wagner Rawling is dead."

Valerie sat up straight. She squeezed the phone. "When? What happened?"

"Yesterday. A boating accident off the Amalfi coast."

"I don't know what to say. I don't even know how I feel about it, except that now Hannah never has a chance to know her grandfather. That's so incredibly sad, Mom."

"Not Wagner, Sr. Junior."

Blood rushed to Valerie's feet. She grabbed the chair cushion and held on. "Her father. Hannah will never know her father."

"He made his bed."

Valerie pressed her fingers against her closed eyes. "One that Hannah and I had to lie in. His choice, and his loss, not knowing his daughter, what a beautiful little girl she is." She opened her eyes and looked around, seeing little. "You don't expect me to come for the funeral, do you?"

"I doubt you would be welcome, since you would have to be explained. And don't think you can get something from his estate. You gave up your rights."

Valerie clenched her teeth. "I know what I did and didn't do, Mom. I don't expect anything. He had more than eight years to make contact, and he didn't. I have no intention of stirring things up."

"Okay. Well, I only told you because you might see it on the news or something, and I didn't want you to be surprised."

"I appreciate that. Is the funeral in Palm Springs or L.A.?"

"L.A. Then Mr. and Mrs. Rawling are coming here for a couple of weeks. They'll probably bring along the young widow."

Valerie forced herself not to react to the reminder that Wagner had married someone else, even before Hannah was born. "You'll be busy."

"That's what I'm paid for."

"Of course."

"Aren't you glad I taught you how to take care of a family? Sounds like you wouldn't have had your cushy new job otherwise."

"Yes, thank you." Yet again. Her mother always reminded her of how much she'd sacrificed for her daughter, and how much wisdom she'd imparted. But Valerie hadn't learned her parenting skills from her. In fact, Valerie had decided to be a very different kind of parent, a more loving one, strict but not unbending, openly affectionate, too. She hadn't gotten many hugs through the years.

Which had also been part of the problem, and a reason why she'd craved Wagner's attention when he offered it. She'd loved being in his arms.

She'd also believed everything he'd told her. Big mistake. Big, big mistake. One she'd paid a heavy price for.

"Well, I've got lots to do here," her mother said. "I'll be talking to you."

Valerie ended the call, then sat back, clutching the phone to her chest. The father-and-child-reunion fantasy was dead. What could she say to Hannah?

She hadn't asked about him in a while, but she would again, at some point. He wasn't real to her, since she'd never met him, but children spun fantasies about such things. How would this affect her?

Valerie tucked the phone back in her pocket. Because David was traveling all day today, she'd agreed to meet Dixie in town for lunch, knowing David wouldn't call with work to do. She drove to the Take a Lode Off Diner.

Dixie hadn't arrived, so Valerie found a table near the window and waited. After a minute she spotted her new friend making her way up the sidewalk, her curls bouncing, looking dressed for comfort in a tank top, jeans and boots, her working wardrobe for her job at a local hardware store owned by her family. The contrast between her outfit and Laura's dress-for-success outfit this morning was huge.

Valerie caught a glimpse of herself reflected in the window, seeing her own dark brown hair pulled back into a ponytail at her nape, knowing the rest of the package included sedate, light blue crop pants, blouse and sandals. She had no curves to speak of, certainly no bustline that brought stares like Dixie's—or Laura's.

Dixie waved after she came through the door and headed to the table, calling out greetings to the other customers and staff. It was what Valerie wished for Hannah, a life in one town, where people knew and looked out for each other. Not that Chance City was tiny, but it was small enough.

"You throw a great party," Dixie said, plucking a menu from the holder beside the mini jukebox.

"Thank you. I like doing that kind of thing."

"I would say it showed, but you never sat down and just enjoyed yourself. You're a worker bee, aren't you?" She raised a hand toward the woman behind the counter. "Honey, can we get a couple of iced teas?"

"Sure thing, Dix."

"Iced tea's okay with you, I hope?"

Valerie nodded.

"You're awful quiet."

Valerie wanted to confide about Wagner dying, but knowing the way gossip got around here, it wouldn't be a secret for long, and she needed it to be a secret, for Hannah's sake. Her daughter needed to fit in.

"I'm sorry," she said as Dixie waited patiently. "A little tired, I guess."

Two glasses of tea were delivered. Dixie sugared hers. "What'd you think of everyone?"

"Very nice people."

Dixie grinned. "You can do better than that. I saw you taking it all in. You quiet types are like that—big thinkers. Mull things around a lot. Don't act without thinking things through."

"That pretty much describes me."

"So, what'd you think of Noah and his brood?"

"Attractive man. Intense. Worries a whole lot about his children but doesn't have a clue about how to parent effectively." Valerie clamped her mouth shut. She shouldn't be talking about her boss's family that way. She looked over the menu, decided on a Cobb salad. Dixie shouted their orders at the counter person.

"We're all worried about Noah," Dixie said. "He loved his wife so much, and he can't seem to get his life back together. I can't tell you how many nannies and housekeepers he's had. Those poor kids." She swirled her straw in her tea. "And Gideon?"

"Didn't get a chance to talk to him." Just overheard some interesting tidbits.

"And Miss Universe?"

Valerie smiled, because she knew it was expected of her. "She's a beautiful woman. She and David complement each other very well."

The bell over the door jangled. "Speak of the devil."

Valerie had her back to the door. "Laura?"

"She's headed our way," Dixie whispered, then leaned over to sip from her straw.

"This is a nice surprise," Laura said, stopping at their table. "I called in a lunch order. May I join you while I wait for it?"

Dixie raised her brows at Valerie, who shrugged slightly.

"Pull up a chair," Dixie said. "I thought you worked in Sacramento on Tuesdays."

"Schedule's always a little off during a holiday week. How's the rest of your morning gone?" she asked Valerie.

"The rest?" Dixie repeated. "You talked today?"

"She dropped by the house this morning."

"Really?" Dixie focused on Laura.

"I wanted her potato salad recipe."

Valerie noted the surprise on Dixie's face. Before Dixie could say anything, Laura added, "She was kind enough to give me the recipe but also her leftovers. Saves me a whole lot of time cooking tonight."

The look Laura gave Dixie intrigued Valerie, something resembling a challenge. Dixie sat back and sipped her iced tea. Valerie figured it was rare that Dixie didn't speak her mind, so it made Valerie even more curious.

Small talk followed. Valerie asked about fun things to do, especially for Hannah, but also as a single woman. Aside from the Stompin' Grounds, there didn't seem to be a whole lot of places to socialize. She could also go to Nevada City or drive down to Sacramento.

She hadn't expected a miracle. She just wanted her life to be interesting and fulfilling…and fun. Yes, she'd missed out on the fun part for too long.

"Laura, your order's up."

She stood. "I've got a client in ten minutes or I'd stay and eat with you," she said, but looked reluctant to leave the two women alone. "Maybe we can do this again sometime."

"O-kay," Dixie said, dragging out the word. Valerie just nodded.

The moment the diner door shut, Dixie leaned toward Valerie. "You were holding out on me. So, Miss Universe paid a call on you this morning, and she wanted your potato salad recipe?"

"Is something wrong with that?"

Dixie started to laugh, then couldn't stop. Finally she sat back, grinning. "The woman can't boil water. She couldn't follow a recipe to save her soul."

Since Valerie had already figured out Laura didn't cook much, that didn't come as much of a surprise.

"Well, I don't think that recipe was what she was after, do you?" Dixie asked.

"No. But I don't have a clue otherwise. Do you?"

"I think she was checkin' out the competition."

"What competition?"

"You."

"But…David told everyone it was just an act he and I had been putting on to help Joseph win you back."

"Heck, Val, I believed it. You fit, you know? And the way you and David ignored each other most of the day yesterday made everyone wonder, too."

"Are you serious?" She felt her face heat. "My job yesterday was to run the party. Why would I socialize with my boss?"

"I'm telling you that we all watched you two dancing together the other night. I don't care what kind of act you think you were puttin' on, there's something there."

"There's nothing there. Nothing. There can't be." Panic set in. She'd just got hired. She couldn't lose the job now, not over gossip. She'd lost her other job over maliciousness. "Dixie, I need you to help me make sure people don't think that about me."

"If I protest too much, it will make everyone even more curious, you know. You don't want to give them more ammunition for gossip."

It was disastrous to Valerie. "So, what do I do now?" On top of the news of Wagner's death, it was almost more than Valerie could handle. Not to mention the fact she *was* attracted to David. She didn't want to leave him— The job. She didn't want to leave the job. And Hannah deserved to live in a nice place and feel safe.

Tears sprang to her eyes.

"Oh, no!" Dixie looked horrified. "I made you cry. I was just having some fun with you. People don't think you and David are having a fling or anything."

"You were joking?"

"I swear I was. Don't be upset."

Dixie didn't know her history, didn't know that the sexual harassment claim still haunted her, still influenced her behavior every day and in every way. But Valerie couldn't share that, either.

She looked down at her empty glass of tea. She wished she had a best girl friend, wished there was someone she could confide in. She was so tired of holding everything in. But until she knew the information wouldn't spread across the gossip network instantly she would keep her secrets.

Even though it had been keeping secrets that had caused so much harm to her life in the past.

"I need to get back to the house," she said, pulling out her wallet. "Hannah will be home before too long."

"You forgive me?" Dixie asked.

Valerie forced a smile. "Of course."

"Good. We can try this again without Laura sometime."

Valerie laughed. "I gathered from your expression that you two aren't friends."

"We're not enemies, but she's living on a different stratosphere from us now. Ex-beauty queen. Lawyer. Rubs elbows with lots of important people these days. When she and David were dating before, we never saw him. She doesn't hang out at the Stompin' Grounds."

Valerie frowned. "You said they broke up months ago. Why was she there yesterday as his date?"

"The million-dollar question. We were all whispering about it at the party."

Valerie couldn't discuss David's love life, so she changed the conversation, then said goodbye and headed home. When the school bus pulled up, she was waiting for her daughter, as usual. Hannah waved to someone before she hopped down the stairs to the ground with a thud.

"Hi!" She grinned ear to ear.

Valerie gave her a hug. They walked up the driveway. "You had a good day?"

"The best. I like it here, Mom. I don't ever want to move."

"I can't guarantee that, but I'll do my best." She slipped an arm around Hannah's shoulders as they stepped inside the cottage. "I have something to tell you."

"What?"

"Let's sit down."

They took a seat on the couch. Valerie held Hannah's hands. "It's been a long time since you asked about your father."

"I know. It always made you sad, so I stopped."

"Well, I heard today that he died."

Hannah's face paled.

"I'm really sorry you never got to meet him."

"Why? He wasn't a nice person, was he? He didn't even want to know me."

"It was more complicated than that, but, yes, he made the decision not to know you. That was his loss, not knowing how beautiful you are, how bright and smart you are. But I know it's a loss for you, too. A loss that can never be made right now. I had hoped that he would change his mind. But, Hannah, you also need to remember that it wasn't about you as a person. His decision not to see you wasn't about you, but about his own inadequacies."

"What does that mean?"

"He didn't have it in him to be a father. It wasn't about you. He would've been the same with any child. If he had known you, I think he couldn't have resisted you."

"Is it okay to be sad? I feel so sad." Her eyes brightened. "And I want to be mad at him."

She took Hannah into her arms and held her. "I know. Yes, you can feel sad or mad or whatever." Someday they would find a special man to love them both.

"I know lots of kids who get new dads. Maybe we can find one, Mom. It would be fun to have a baby brother."

Valerie kissed the top of Hannah's head and smiled. She wouldn't mind that herself.

Except this time she wanted to have a husband holding her hand while she gave birth.

Chapter Ten

Home. The refuge David had created for himself beckoned as he pulled into his driveway. He'd been gone three and a half long, exhausting weeks. In his briefcase were orders for twelve more cars. Four were for repeat customers, who'd required only a little wining and dining before signing on the dotted lines. The others were new, a couple of the men playing David against a competitor to try to drive down the price or add expensive options free. But David believed that if he cheapened the business by cutting the price, he cheapened himself. He'd nailed the deals by emphasizing quality and customer service, as he always did.

Valerie's car was in its place in the garage. He felt his tension ease further. This was what he needed—to be home, where life was peaceful. It was Saturday, so he would have the rest of the weekend to relax and had told Noah he was taking a couple more days off. He wanted to lie around the pool, visit friends, hang out with the guys.

He wanted to let Valerie take care of the details of his life for a little while.

She wasn't to be found, however, not in the kitchen or the living room, at least. He set his luggage on the bottom step of the staircase, then headed to his office to leave his brief-case. He could hear singing as he neared the room.

He reached the doorway. Hannah was there, a duster in her hand, singing and dancing around the room, flicking surfaces. She stopped cold when she saw him. Belle barked a greeting and hurried up to him.

"What are you doing?" he asked, scratching the dog's ears. He'd specifically told Valerie that Hannah could not work in his house. He'd expected her to honor his wishes.

"Don't tell my mom, please," Hannah begged. "Pleeease."

"She doesn't know you're here?"

"She knows I'm in the big house, but I'm supposed to be doing homework in the dining room. The cable's out on the television, so she's with the man in the cottage while he works on it."

David had noticed the van in front of the house but hadn't given it a second thought.

Hannah inched closer. Belle moved to stand beside her, as if protecting her. "I know I'm not supposed to be here. I won't do it again, I promise. Just don't tell Mom."

He wasn't knowledgeable about the inner workings of kids' minds, except for having been a kid himself. "You know she doesn't want you working, Hannah, so why did you do it?"

"I wasn't working. I was dusting. I love to dust. It's fun."

"What's fun about it?"

"Oh, you know. Making swirls. Writing your name. Except Mom doesn't usually let enough dust pile up to do much. But I like it. I get to dust the cottage."

"And you like to dance, apparently."

Her eyes lit up. "It's the best."

"Do you take lessons?"

"Someday. Mom promised."

"Well, your mom probably heard my car arrive, so you'd better get to where you're supposed to be before she catches you herself."

"Are you going to tell her?"

"Don't you think *you* should?"

"Only if I do it again." Her smile was beguiling.

"Go on," he said, not giving her an answer, but grinning as she raced out of the room, Belle on her heels. Such drama over a small disobeying of the rules. He guessed little girls were like that, though.

He decided to head to the cottage and check out the cable situation himself. He passed the dining room, countered Hannah's bright smile with a stern look and a gesture to get back to her homework, then walked to the cottage.

The front door was open. He could hear Valerie laughing inside. David stopped before he came into view, listening. Was she flirting? Yeah, definitely a flirtatious lilt to her voice.

He frowned. He wasn't paying her to flirt on the job. How—

He stopped the thought. She was entitled to a social life, although she never mentioned having one, and they'd talked every day. She was always home when he called.

Before David could make his presence known, someone came out the door, the cable guy. He was big, burly, bearded and over sixty. And David had known him all his life. He'd been the baseball coach for his Little League teams for years.

"Heya, Dave."

"Rodney." They shook hands. "You working Saturdays now?"

"We alternate. Emergencies only. Got you all fixed up."

Valerie came up beside him and smiled at David, her eyes…glowing. He'd never felt so welcomed. He took a step toward her then stopped. He'd almost hugged her.

"You're home," she said, looking pleased.

His last bit of lingering tension melted away. "Yeah. So, what was wrong with the cable?"

"Water and rust," Rodney said. "Old lines."

"Only five years."

"Old by today's standards. Job security." Rodney winked. He passed a clipboard to Valerie and pointed to where she needed to sign for the work done. "I'm off. Got a few more stops to make."

"Good seeing you, Rod," David said.

"Thank you!" Valerie called to his back, getting an over-the-shoulder wave in return as he trudged off. She clasped her hands in front of her. David realized she did that whenever she wanted to keep things professional between them. Her "employee" pose. "How was your trip home?" she asked.

"No different from any other. The yard looks good. I think I see a few flowers in bloom that weren't there before."

She looked a little guilty. "Just some purple sage."

He noticed she didn't apologize or justify. "I didn't know their name."

She glanced around. "Joseph has begrudgingly let me tend much of the garden. He does all the heavy and tedious stuff."

"Do you ever rest?"

She blinked in surprise. "Gardening relaxes me."

"If you say so. Does Hannah help?"

She put a hand to her mouth. "Hannah. She's in your dining room doing homework. I'll go get her."

She started past him. He put a hand on her arm to stop her, then didn't let go. Her skin was warm and soft.

"She can stay until she's done. Interrupting her might not be the best thing," he said, releasing her because he felt her arm tense up.

"If you're sure." Her voice was tight, pitched a little higher than usual. "Normally she's not allowed in the house at all, except the kitchen. I want you to know I don't let her violate the privacy of your space."

Little do you know. "I trust you." Although he wasn't too sure about her daughter.

She cocked her head. "You must be exhausted."

"Understatement."

"Are you hungry? Could I fix you lunch?"

She's paid to take care of you. Let her. "Yes, thanks."

They walked back to the house in silence, yet he was completely aware of her. *Absence makes the heart—*

"I'm going to take a swim," he said, knowing he had to distance himself right away.

"Should I bring your lunch down to the pool?"

"Yeah, thanks." He strode through the kitchen, grabbed his luggage from the bottom step and took the stairs to his bedroom, two at a time. He tossed his luggage on his bed. Valerie would take care of it later.

It didn't take him long to change into a swimsuit and T-shirt. He grabbed a towel, then the phone rang.

"You're home."

He sat in an overstuffed chair, dragged a hand down his face and tucked the phone closer. "Hi, Laura."

Valerie glanced at the Caller ID on the kitchen phone when it rang. Laura Bannister. She hadn't wasted any time. Or maybe he'd called her from the road. Maybe she would zip into the driveway in that fancy red Miata, haul her bikini-clad perfect body out of it and loll by the pool with David all afternoon.

Valerie sniffed. If David told her to stay away from the house, that he wanted privacy…

He has every right. The booming voice in her head irritated her because it spoke the truth. He did have every right. It was just that she'd begun to feel proprietary—about the house and the yard and even about him. The time they spent on the phone every day had taken on an importance she shouldn't have allowed. But once the business was discussed and handled, the conversation usually turned personal, if only for a little while. Most of the time he called after he was in his hotel room for the night and almost ready for bed, an hour when Hannah was in school.

Day by day Valerie had heard the increasing weariness in his voice, making her wish she'd been free to travel with him, to help with the load somehow.

Liar. The honest voice in her head took her to task. She just liked being with him. The time apart hadn't been easy, but she'd done her best to expand her social circle. She'd gone to the Stompin' Grounds twice with Dixie and Joseph, had danced a lot, but no one asked her out. She had a sinking feeling that people still didn't believe she and David had been putting on a show that night, that she didn't belong to him. The men were friendly, but kept her at a respectful distance.

Not that she'd wanted to date any of them. But still, it would be nice to be asked.

She grabbed some deli roast beef from the refrigerator and threw together a sandwich for David, adding macaroni salad, sliced cantaloupe and a chocolate-chip cookie to the plate.

The phone-line light went out. Ended. Not a long conversation. Because she was on the way over?

"I'm done," Hannah said, coming in and pulling a cookie from the jar, her homework tucked in her arms. "Can I swim now?"

"Mr. Falcon is going to use the pool. Maybe later. You need to get on down to the cottage and clean up your bedroom before Gabby gets here." It was going to be Hannah's first sleepover.

Valerie heard David pad down the staircase. She and Hannah both turned toward the kitchen doorway as he came through. His gaze connected with Hannah's. She looked down and shuffled her feet. He seemed to be challenging her with his eyes.

Valerie frowned. What was going on? "Is there...something I should know about, Hannah?" she asked.

Play the Lucky Hearts Game

and get...

2 FREE BOOKS and
2 FREE MYSTERY GIFTS...
YOURS to KEEP!

yes! I have scratched off the silver card. Please send me my *2 FREE BOOKS* and *2 FREE mystery GIFTS* (gifts are worth about $10). I understand that I am under no obligation to purchase any books as explained on the back of this card.

Scratch Here!

then look below to see what your cards get you... 2 Free Books & 2 Free Mystery Gifts!

335 SDL ESTX   235 SDL ESXA

FIRST NAME

LAST NAME

ADDRESS

APT.#

CITY

STATE / PROV.

ZIP / POSTAL CODE

(S-SE-07/08)

Twenty-one gets you
2 FREE BOOKS and
2 FREE MYSTERY GIFTS!

Twenty gets you
2 FREE BOOKS!

Nineteen gets you
1 FREE BOOK!

TRY AGAIN!

If offer card is missing write to: The Silhouette Reader Service, 3010 Walden Ave., P.O. Box 1867, Buffalo, NY 14240-1867

BUSINESS REPLY MAIL
FIRST-CLASS MAIL   PERMIT NO. 717   BUFFALO, NY

POSTAGE WILL BE PAID BY ADDRESSEE

SILHOUETTE READER SERVICE
3010 WALDEN AVE
PO BOX 1867
BUFFALO NY 14240-9952

NO POSTAGE
NECESSARY
IF MAILED
IN THE
UNITED STATES

"No." The answer came too fast and strong.

Yes, there was. Valerie knew when her daughter was lying, but she would ask her again in private, wouldn't confront David about it until she knew what she was dealing with and there was definitely something. "Get going now, Hannah."

She scurried out, snatching another cookie on her way and grinning at her mother. They'd had a difficult few weeks since learning her father had died, with Hannah alternating between sad and mad, so to see her smile now was a relief. Still...that didn't mean she would be allowed to keep secrets. Secrets hurt too much when they were revealed.

David picked up the lunch plate, grabbed a beer from the refrigerator and started to leave without comment.

"Will you be home for dinner?" she asked.

He stopped at the door. "No, don't plan anything for me."

When the door shut behind him, she stared at the countertop. A date with Laura? Would he be gone all night?

She didn't like the feelings that swamped her at the thought of them together. She'd seen Laura twice more while he was gone. Once she'd stopped by to bring Valerie some wonderful bakery cookies as a thank-you for the potato salad, and the other with Dixie at the diner again, the timing coincidental—or so Valerie thought. Both times Laura was friendly but curious, asking an occasional question about David, ones she should've known the answer to already. Small talk, Valerie had thought.

She gave David enough time to eat, then went down to the patio to pick up his dishes to put away before she headed to the cottage for Gabby's arrival. He hadn't gotten in the pool, but had eaten then fallen asleep on a chaise lounge wearing just his swimsuit, looking like every woman's dream—except for the lines of exhaustion on his face, even in sleep. She stood watching him, wondering how she could make his life easier.

He opened his eyes. Not asleep, after all. Caught staring at him, she did nothing, not risking letting him see how flustered she was at being caught. He stared back for several seconds, his gaze intense.

"You're blocking my sun," he said finally.

She picked up his plate and the empty bottle. "Can I bring you another?"

"No, thanks."

"I'll be in the cottage if you need me. Hannah's friend Gabby is spending the night."

"Okay."

She started to turn around.

"Valerie?"

"Yes?" She waited and waited but he said nothing, keeping her in suspense. "If that's all, then?"

"I wanted to thank you for your great work. You made my job a whole lot easier."

Music to her ears. "I'm so glad. Thank you for saying so. You're the best boss I've ever had." She hurried off before he saw how affected she was by his words. She'd spent a whole year without being praised, without being recognized for her job skills and work ethic. Even her mother hadn't offered encouragement but constantly made Valerie aware of her failings.

A few minutes later she walked into Hannah's room as she struggled to make her bed. "What's going on?" she asked her daughter, going to the other side of the bed to help.

"Nothing."

"You're keeping a secret."

"No, I'm not." She tugged hard at the blanket, pulling it out of the foot of the bed.

Valerie eyed her. She trusted David, had no reason not to, but she knew her daughter. "Is Mr. Falcon…treating you okay?"

"What do you mean?" She kept working at the bedding instead of looking at Valerie.

"You know what I mean. We've talked about it before. If an adult does something—"

"No! Mom, no. He's cool." Hannah finally looked her in the eye, which made Valerie believe her.

"Just remember you can tell me anything, okay? Anything."

"I *knooow*."

"Okay."

Later in the evening she heard his car pull out of the garage. The girls were immersed in a DVD but doing more talking than listening. "How about a swim?" she asked. The late-September evenings cooled quickly. They wouldn't be able to swim for much longer.

"Yay!" They'd been wearing their bathing suits for a couple of hours, waiting for their opportunity, and headed out the door instantly, tangling arms, legs and bodies in their hurry, giggling.

Valerie brought her glass of iced tea and sat on a lounge, watching them. Evenings were hardest on her. It was the hour when all across the country families were sitting down to dinner together. Okay, so maybe that was a bit of a stretch. Times had changed. Life wasn't like those old sitcoms anymore, where families gathered to talk and laugh over their evening meal. Everyone was busy with soccer and baseball and gymnastics, moms and dads chauffeuring constantly, grabbing meals on the run, getting home in time for homework, baths and bedtime.

But Valerie longed for that fantasy. It'd been only her and her mother for eighteen years. Now her and Hannah. They did eat their meals together, at least so far. But Valerie wanted the whole package, an entire family around the dinner table. Including a husband.

The longing for that ideal had begun to invade her dreams, waking her up at night, a steady thumping in the hollows of her heart, aching. It had probably intensified lately because of Wagner's death. Even though they never would have married, he'd always been the placeholder in her dreams, the possibility, as Hannah's father. Now there were no possibilities.

Except…David had materialized now instead, hazy but undeniably there, waking her from a sound sleep, tempting her.

And she'd promised him if he hired her that she wouldn't run off and get married or have a baby anytime soon. She wouldn't go back on her word, even though she wanted that dream of home and family.

When she saw Hannah's and Gabby's lips turning blue, she made them get out of the pool and into the hot tub, then served them spaghetti and meatballs in the cottage and popcorn later as they finished their movie. They stayed up for hours in Hannah's bedroom, giggling and whispering.

Valerie didn't order them to sleep but let them wear themselves out, the clock striking midnight when they finally gave in. She wandered out into the yard and let the cold air wash over her. Ever since David had gotten home, she'd been agitated. And frustrated. Excited. Tense.

Happy.

She heard his car ease up the driveway, got caught in the beam of his headlights before he disappeared into the garage.

The night seemed extraordinarily dark and quiet as he approached.

"You okay?" he asked.

"The girls finally fell asleep. I was unwinding before bed." The domestic moment relaxed her. "Did you have a good evening?"

"It was okay." He slid his hands into his pockets. "Just trying to stay awake long enough to adjust to California time again. Another Saturday night at the Stompin' Grounds. I'm taking Monday and Tuesday off, too. I don't think I told you."

"No, but that's no problem. I adjust to whatever you need."

"I won't be working. Not sure what I'm going to do, but Falcon Motorcars can function without me for a couple of days." He lifted a hand toward her, lightly touching her forearm. "You're cold."

She'd been rubbing her arms without thinking about it. "Nippy nights."

"You should get inside."

"In a minute." It was easier to talk to him in the dark. "I know something happened between Hannah and you."

A beat passed. "What did she say?"

"She didn't, except to say it wasn't something I should worry about."

"It isn't, but I told her she should tell you, not me. Why don't we wait and see what happens. It's not a big deal, Valerie. Truly, it is not a big deal at all."

"I promised you she wouldn't interfere in your life."

"She didn't. Don't worry about it."

She couldn't help but worry, especially since she didn't know what *it* was.

"If it gets to be an issue and she doesn't tell you," he said, "I will."

"Good."

An awkward silence ensued. "I'll see you in the morning," he said. "I'll get my own breakfast. Joe and I are going to do a little power biking early."

"Do you want me to pack a lunch?"

"We'll stop somewhere. Good night."

"Good night. I'm glad you're home." She walked away, even though she would rather have sat by the pool for a while. She figured he needed to know she was safely in the cottage before he went to bed himself.

I'm glad you're home. Simple words, David thought as he lay in bed a while later. Home. He'd missed it more than ever. It was the longest he'd been away in years. Noah must figure that since Valerie was there to take care of things, David could be gone even longer. But living out of a suitcase, always being "on" for clients, had lost its appeal. It wasn't fun anymore.

He needed to have it out with Noah. Gideon was right,

pointing out what Noah, and even David himself, hadn't seen. He'd hit breaking point. He was almost thirty years old. He needed a life beyond work. With all the new orders, the company could afford to hire a Europe-based sales rep, although that would alter David's place in the company, as well. He'd have to give it all some thought, see how he could shift company priorities somehow so that he remained challenged by the job but not worn-out.

He tucked his hands behind his head. Noah was so much like their father—in charge, in control, his views about everything almost unchangeable. *Almost.* That was the key word. David just had to have a plan. One that would keep him at home more but also not require Noah to be gone, either. Something win-win. But would Noah trust an outsider to drum up business at the European end? Their father had started the business. They'd never had someone outside the family take on a major role.

His thoughts swirling, unable to sleep, David grabbed the remote and turned on the television, flipping through channels until he came across a show about the history of the American Le Mans series.

The TV was still on when he woke up, and a note-filled pad on the floor beside him. It had been a long, busy night.

Chapter Eleven

"Go to a dinner party? With *you?*" Valerie made herself sit, instead of plop, in a chair in front of David's desk the next afternoon after he'd issued the invitation—or perhaps *edict* was a better word. He'd pretty much told her she would accompany him, not asked.

"You don't have to look so horrified," he said, leaning back.

She schooled her features. "I'm just surprised."

"Right. As I said, it's a business dinner."

What about Laura? She didn't say the words aloud. His personal life was just that. "Why me?" she said instead.

"I want a second opinion of these men. You'd be neutral. Plus you'll probably pick up on things I wouldn't."

"How dressy will it be?"

"I've heard most women have the little black dress. Something like that."

She didn't have one, but didn't want to admit it. And she'd splurged enough lately on Hannah and even herself that she didn't want to charge anything else, if at all possible. Her savings account was just starting to grow again.

"If you don't have anything," David said, "I'll assume the expense. It's for the job, after all."

She lifted her chin. "That won't be necessary."

"Okay. So, tomorrow night. We should leave here by five-thirty for Sacramento. You'll need a babysitter."

"I'll take care of it." She had to go shopping. Would she find something appropriate in Chance City or have to go elsewhere? How much could she charge before her credit card would deny it? Were the right stores open on Sunday?

"So, you don't get to take a little vacation, after all," she said, because he was examining her too closely.

"I'm still not going into the office." He steepled his fingers in front of his face. "You look upset, Valerie."

Not much escaped him. "I'm just surprised. I didn't figure this kind of thing would be part of my job description." *Why aren't you taking Laura?*

"I'll make sure to add it officially." He smiled slightly. "It hadn't occurred to me, either. You're okay with it, though, right?"

Like she had a choice? "Yes, of course. Is that all?"

"You sure you want to do it?"

"I'm fine with it." She left his office and headed to the cottage. Hannah was at Gabby's house. Valerie was supposed to pick her up after dinner, which meant she had about two hours to shop. She called Dixie and asked where she might find a little black dress.

"A friend of mine runs a consignment shop. Why don't I give her a call? See what she's got on hand," Dixie said.

"That would be great, thanks."

"Have a hot date, do you?"

"A business meeting to attend with David, that's all." She hung up still wondering why he wanted her along. Laura was impressive, in looks and brains. Valerie was just…ordinary.

Then the realization struck her. Laura might be a distraction to the business at hand. She was too beautiful and too naturally sexy. David would need to keep the focus on himself and the business. No one would look twice at Valerie. She was *safe*.

Now that she'd figured out her role, she relaxed.

Dixie called back. "Surie says she's got a couple of things that might work for you. Want me to meet you there? Give my objective opinion?"

"Oh, yes, thanks. I need to pick up Hannah at six o'clock, though."

"Store'll be closed by then, anyway." She gave Valerie directions. "See you there."

Later, when Valerie got home and hung up her purchase in anticipation of the dinner the next night, she sat on her bed and stared at the dress. Had she made a mistake? Should she have gone for something high-necked and long-sleeved instead of the sleeveless, scooped-but-not-too-much-cleavage-revealing neckline? Of course, she didn't have a whole lot of cleavage to expose, anyway, so it was hardly an issue.

She sighed. If it wasn't right, she would know it by the look on his face the next night, and she'd picked another more sedate dress to have as a backup, figuring she could return one or the other.

Hannah came into the room, dressed in her pajamas, all warm and sweet from a shower. She sat next to Valerie on the bed and looked at the dress hanging in plain sight.

"That's pretty, Mom."

"Thanks. I like it, too." She slipped an arm around her daughter and held her close, kissing her damp hair.

"Where are you going?"

"To a dinner meeting with Mr. Falcon tomorrow night, and it's kind of formal. Aggie's going to come watch you."

"Cool."

She was quiet long enough that Valerie wondered if she was working up the nerve to talk about whatever the issue was with David, but she said nothing.

"Did you have fun this weekend with Gabby?"

"Yeah."

The way Hannah said the word made Valerie wonder. "But?" she prompted.

Hannah moved away a little. "Her dad's really funny."

"Isn't that a good thing?"

"I wish I had a dad like that."

The yearning in her voice made Valerie ache. "I know you do, honey. Maybe someday. We have to meet the right man."

"You need to be going on dates, Mom. You can't find the right man unless you go where guys go."

Valerie smiled at her grown-up little girl. "I'll put more effort into it."

"Gabby's got a real family. Her little brother and sister are kind of bratty, but they're kind of fun, too."

Well, pile on the guilt, why don't you, dear daughter? She pulled Hannah to her feet and headed to her bedroom to tuck her in. Valerie had missed having a traditional family, too, growing up. She understood the longing to be like other families, even if "real families" were all different kinds of mixes these days. She certainly considered her and Hannah a real family, just not the old stereotypical fifties-sitcom kind.

Valerie pulled out her finances folder and a calculator, then sat at the kitchen counter to examine the documents. She had two more car payments, then that debt would be gone. Then she'd tackle the big bill, her credit card. She calculated how soon she could pay it off. Even keeping her expenses to the bare necessities, it would take a year.

She'd been putting money into savings, even though she should add on to her payments, but she needed the security of cash in the bank, too. She would never let herself get into that tenuous financial position again.

Which meant she had to work a little harder at keeping David at a distance, physically. And emotionally, which was even more dangerous, especially when they were going on a—

Not a date. They weren't going on a date tomorrow. She needed to keep remembering that.

As they drove home from Sacramento the next night, Valerie sat quietly, thinking about the evening, starting from the moment he'd shown up at her door with Aggie.

"You look nice," she'd said before she could censor herself. "I've never seen you in a suit before."

"So do you."

"Thanks." She'd figured he was just being polite, returning a compliment, and yet his gaze lingered on her, looking surprised, then appreciative, if she was reading him right. She'd hurried past him to the garage, wanting to reestablish their professional relationship, unable to stop herself from sneaking glances at him now and then as they made the trip, admiring the way he handled the Falcon. How his wrist rested on the steering wheel, how capably he drove, how relaxed he was.

He'd briefed her on the two men and their wives they would be having dinner with, as well as on the idea he had, one he wouldn't share with his brother until it was a done deal except for signing on the dotted line. David was trusting her to keep his plan secret until then.

But the evening had been mostly social, a getting-to-know-you occasion. David would have a sit-down with both men before the week was up.

Social, indeed, Valerie thought. David had even been social with *her*.

She looked out the passenger window and rubbed her arms, remembering the times he'd touched her during the evening—his fingers pressing the small of her back as they walked through the restaurant, brushing her arm during dinner, even tucking her hair back when the Delta breezes had swirled while they waited outdoors for the car to be brought around. She'd gone on alert, getting more confused about her role with every gesture. He'd made it seem to the other people as if they were lovers.

"I'd appreciate your thoughts," he said to her now, giving her a quick glance as they moved along the freeway toward home.

She pulled herself together. "Mr. Peterson seems straightforward. And he adores his wife. He has character. Mr. Koning? I can't say the same. And they're business partners? It's hard to believe."

"Peterson's the money man. Koning would be responsible for the details of the project. This wouldn't be his first time. Proven track record."

She frowned. "He seems rigid to me. He also keeps his wife on a short leash."

"Meaning what? I noticed she drank a lot."

"The Petersons noticed, too, and didn't approve. So, does Mr. Koning have her on a leash because she drinks a lot? Or is it vice versa? I know you said he's had a lot of success with this kind of project, but I'd hesitate to involve someone I didn't fully trust."

"Thanks. I appreciate the input."

She caught him eyeing her low neckline for just a moment. Heat zapped her, head to toe, as it had many times during the evening. How little it took to arouse her...

"You were a great asset tonight, Valerie."

"I was nervous."

"It didn't show."

Her confusion increased at the tone of his voice, soft, almost seductive. "I need to ask you a question," she said.

"Shoot."

"Why didn't you introduce me as your assistant? Everyone assumed I was your girlfriend."

"It was a social meeting. At least on the surface. I don't want them to know the specifics of the project until I decide they're the people I want for the job."

"So, why didn't you take Laura?"

He frowned. "Why would I?"

"Well, she's your girlfriend. And she's definitely an asset."

"What makes you think she's my girlfriend?"

Valerie clamped her mouth shut. Had she heard him correctly? "Isn't she? You brought her to your Labor Day party."

"As a decoy. You told me I had to bring a date so that people wouldn't think you and I were an item."

"Hold on. I'm really confused. You date her, right?"

"I used to. She ended it."

"Then…I don't understand. And I know it's none of my business, either."

He took the freeway exit and headed toward home. "She agreed to come as a favor, that's all."

But she talks as if you're together. "That wasn't her only reason for doing it." She closed her eyes. She had no right saying that to him, trying to force a confidence.

He blew out a breath. "Yeah, you're right. She wanted to pick things up again. I had to end it."

He ended it? She really wasn't his girlfriend? "When did that happen?"

"Right before she headed home after the party." He turned into the driveway, then stopped in front of the garage, since he still had to take Aggie home. He turned off the engine and angled toward her. "I haven't mentioned her to you since, have I? Why did you think the relationship was continuing?"

The dark night enveloped them. Knowing they may never speak so personally again, Valerie wanted to continue the conversation, to learn the truth. She couldn't tell him about Laura trying to get information out of her, though. She didn't want any scenes because of it. But Valerie remembered seeing them hug after the party, too. So, it was a goodbye hug? "I just assumed, I guess. She's certainly your type."

"What would that be?"

"Beautiful. Smart." Probably great in bed. Valerie didn't have enough experience to know whether the same could be said of herself.

"You're more my type." He touched her shoulder, a feathery whisper of fingertips against her skin, then pulled away abruptly, grabbing the steering wheel and looking straight ahead. "I apologize. That was way out of line."

Out of line, maybe, but it felt nice. A little sinful. Forbidden. "It fit the evening, I guess, which has been unpredictable for me."

"It wasn't…appropriate behavior."

His irritation at himself calmed her. She was glad he was struggling with the attraction, too. Was it just proximity? The fact he didn't currently have a girlfriend? Or was it specifically her?

It was crazy to even be thinking about him in that way. Crazy. She'd promised herself she wouldn't do anything to mess up the best job she'd ever had. And even just admitting there were feelings could mess it up. Giving in to them definitely *would* mess it up.

She felt his gaze on her, and anticipation in the air, hot and palpable. They'd been playing at the whole boyfriend/girlfriend thing all evening. If she'd been aroused by it, he could be, too. In fact, seemed to be, if she could judge by his unsteady breathing. She wanted to touch him. He'd touched her but she hadn't done so in return, confused by his attention and not knowing exactly what role she was supposed to be playing.

Now she wanted—needed—to touch him, if just for a moment. He'd taken off his jacket and rolled up his shirt-sleeves before they'd driven away from the restaurant. His forearms looked strong and sinewy. Tempting. She rested her fingers on his arm.

He turned to her in an instant, slid a hand behind her neck and pulled her to meet him. He stopped, his mouth an inch from hers.

"This is a stupid idea," he said.

"Yes." Her heart thundered.

He didn't move. "You look beautiful tonight. And very sexy." Her pulse went supersonic. "I'm glad you think so."

"I had a hard time keeping my eyes off you."

She waited, letting him dictate what would happen. She

should be saying no, loudly, adamantly. The word stayed stuck in her throat.

"This is really stupid," he repeated, but he didn't wait for her response this time, settling his mouth on hers, taking the kiss deep right away, his tongue searching, arousing. She groaned, giving back with everything she had, giving in to the feelings that had been building since she'd met him, her knight, her rescuer. She tried not to think of him in those terms, but it was useless. He was all that to her. He'd changed her life in every possible way.

And now she could taste him, put her hands on him and feel him, hold him...

He stopped, moved back slightly, his hand still cupping her neck. "Damn."

Valerie panicked at the word. It had started already, the regret. They'd ruined—

"I've been wanting to do that for a long time," he said, soft and gruff.

"You have?"

"Yeah."

"I don't want to complicate our relationship, our business relationship, David."

"I know." He brushed his thumb along her jaw.

"Please don't fire me."

He dropped his hand. "I have no intention of firing you."

"You can't sleep with me, either. We can't go there at all. We can't kiss again. I can't lose this job, David. I can't."

His gaze held steady. "Can you forget this happened?"

"I have to, okay?" She was so wrong to have given in to her feelings, her needs. "I have to. So do you." She grabbed the door handle. "I'll send Aggie out."

He didn't stop her, either with words or action. She hurried to the cottage, then paused outside the door long enough to calm herself. She put her hand on the doorknob, twisted it open, stepped inside.

Aggie looked up from the television, then shoved herself up off the sofa.

"Did you have a good time?" she asked.

Valerie nodded. "How was Hannah?"

"An angel, as always." Aggie started to walk past then stopped and scrutinized Valerie's face. After a moment she nodded. "G'night."

Valerie shivered at the straightforward, soul-searching look Aggie gave her. When the door shut, Valerie pulled out her cell phone. She'd gotten a voice message earlier in the evening that she'd ignored because it hadn't identified the caller.

She punched the buttons to retrieve the voice mail.

"Valerie, this is Wagner Rawling, Sr."

Valerie reached blindly for the sofa and dropped into it, gripping the phone.

"I need to talk to you. I don't care how late it is." He left his number, then ended the call.

The last time she'd heard from him was when she'd graduated from business school, more than six years ago. He'd come to make sure she'd completed the courses he'd paid for. Since then, silence.

She set down the phone as if it were on fire. Wagner Rawling, Sr., he said. Maybe he thought she didn't know his son had died. He sounded as arrogant as she remembered.

Yes, arrogant—except for when his son had slept with the housekeeper's daughter and gotten her pregnant. Then Senior, as the family called him, had gone from merely superior to despot.

Valerie couldn't stand up to him then. She'd been eighteen and scared to death. But now? Now she was older and wiser and not so easily pushed around.

She closed her eyes. Her mother had to be involved in whatever he wanted, since she was the only one who knew her phone number.

Valerie put her phone on the charger, turned off the lights

and went to bed, knowing she wouldn't sleep, but determined not to let him think she would jump when he snapped his fingers. Not now. Not ever again. She was not returning his call tonight. Maybe not ever.

As she lay in bed ignoring Senior, her thoughts turned to David, which didn't ease her mind, either. She'd messed up, big-time. Even though he said he wouldn't fire her, the kiss would change their relationship forever.

And probably not for good.

Just when everything was going so well…

Chapter Twelve

David settled in a deck chair the next morning, coffee mug in hand, newspaper on the table, the rubber band still in place. He waved back to Hannah as she danced—there was no other word for it—up the driveway to wait for the school bus. Valerie followed a few seconds later, not looking in his direction.

Not a good sign.

He probably should regret that he'd kissed her, but he rarely regretted any life experience. Experience was just that—something to try out, declare a failure or success, then file in your memory.

Yet regret over kissing her niggled at him. Not the actual kissing, since that was damn good, but her reaction afterward, and the sure-to-follow tension in their relationship.

He'd spent a lot of time watching her at dinner, enjoying the way she seemed so interested in everyone and their conversations, appreciating an occasional brush of their arms for the surprising little jolt of reaction. Hearing her laugh, a fairly rare occurrence, although she smiled a lot, more with her eyes than her mouth.

Unlike Laura, who exuded sex appeal all the time, Valerie was more girl-next-door and yet even sexier to him, even with the unrevealing clothing she usually wore. Which had made last night's exception so interesting. She'd definitely shown more skin than she ever had before.

In only six weeks she'd somehow become important in every aspect of his life.

Which was a big complication.

He heard the kitchen door open and shut, then she opened the slider to the deck.

"Good morning," she said, her hands folded in front of her.

"Hey."

"Have you eaten breakfast?"

"No. Have you?" He couldn't read her. She seemed calm, until he looked at her eyes. And then he noticed her fidgeting a little, rare for her.

"Yes. Would you like an omelet?"

He wanted to keep her nearby, maybe get a chance to clear the air. "Sure. Thanks." She made great omelets now that she was doing the shopping and had actual ingredients on hand, not just what was left over in his refrigerator from his own occasional shopping trip.

She shut the door, turning away. He opened the newspaper and scanned the headlines. After a minute she came out onto the porch, a portable phone in her hand. She wore her apron, which still had the power to turn him on.

"Noah wants to talk to you."

"Tell him I'm on vacation for one more day."

She relayed the message, then listened. "He says it's urgent."

"Everything is urgent to Noah." He went back to reading his paper.

"Is there blood involved?" Valerie said into the phone.

"No one's in the hospital?... In jail?... Then he's not avail able, Noah."

David raised his brows and smiled. She smiled back.

"Thanks," he said when she pushed the off button.

"He said he sent you an e-mail."

"Well, damn. My e-mail is going to be down all day."

She smiled a little wider. "What *are* you going to do with your day off?"

"I'm thinking about going to a movie."

"Really?"

She didn't add, "Alone?" but he heard the word, anyway. "Yeah." He grabbed the entertainment section. "Wanna go with me? We'll go to an early matinee and be home in time for Hannah's bus."

"That would be a date, David. You know we can't do that."

"What if I make it a job responsibility for the day?" Well, that was pathetic. Order her to go with him. Cool.

"Then I would go. I'd take my steno pad and my PDA and await orders."

She said it in a light tone, but he heard her frustration.

"I enjoy your company, Valerie."

"I'm your employee."

He stood.

She took a step back. "I need to finish fixing your break-fast." She shut the door in his face.

Skittish. He wondered if he'd ever used that word before. Not out loud, for sure, but even in his mind? It described her perfectly, but it wouldn't have been part of his definition of her until now. And he'd caused it.

Well, hell, she'd kissed him back. Gave it her all, it felt like.

Edgy, he moved to lean against the railing, surveying his yard. Soon she opened the door and said his breakfast was ready.

He didn't turn around. "I see yellow flowers."

"Do you?" came the innocent-sounding response.

"I remember specifically saying no flowers. Now I've got purple and yellow ones."

"The garden looks nice, doesn't it? The color gives your eyes someplace to linger. Your breakfast is getting cold."

He turned to look at her and saw worry in her expression. Because of the flower business? Because she really was worried about losing her job?

Her cell phone rang. Her face paled.

"Aren't you going to answer that?" he asked.

"I'll check it later." Tension coated her words, making her voice tight.

"What if it's about Hannah?"

She slipped the phone out of her pocket and looked at the screen. "It isn't." She tucked the phone away. "I'll be back in a little while to clean up."

He got inside the kitchen in time to see the back door close behind her. After weeks of predictable behavior, she was all of a sudden…not behaving predictably. She'd shown more varied emotion this one morning than the rest of the time put together.

What was happening? She looked worried. No, beyond worried—scared.

It couldn't all have to do with the kiss, so what else was happening?

And how could he find out?

"Why is Mr. Rawling calling me, Mom?" Valerie had tucked her feet up in a chair, making herself small, as she called her mother after Senior phoned a second time, and Valerie had ignored his call a second time.

"I don't know."

"He had to have gotten my number from you."

"Yes. He asked for it and I gave it. But I don't know what he wants. He's my boss, Valerie. I don't ask questions."

"You should've called me and let me be the one doing the calling. I don't like him having my number."

"A man like him can get any number he wants."

She was probably right about that. Valerie rubbed her forehead.

"Please call him back," her mother begged. "He's already upset with me because you haven't."

"Why should he be upset with *you?* I'm an adult. You have no control over me."

"In his world, the parent always has control, you know? I have to go now," she whispered in a rush. "I hear the missus coming."

Valerie pushed the off button but didn't move. She didn't want her mother to be in trouble, but she also didn't want to talk to the man. It couldn't be good news.

She pressed her hands to her face. Her life had just settled into a good rhythm. She didn't want anything disrupting it. Especially now that Hannah had stopped talking about her father.

But Valerie knew Senior would find a way to get to her, probably even track her down here at David's house. She couldn't have that.

She blew out a shaky breath and dialed his number. Her stomach roiled.

"Hello, Valerie," he said amiably.

"Mr. Rawling."

"Long time."

Not long enough. "Yes, sir."

"Your mother told you about my son?"

"Yes, sir. I'm very sorry for your loss." Tears suddenly burned her eyes and throat. She hadn't given in to grief until this moment, the grief of a mother for her child who would never know her father. The grief of an eighteen-year-old girl for her first love, who'd never loved her back but had given her a child she cherished, one she couldn't imagine life without. For that she had always been grateful to fate for sending Wagner her way.

"I hadn't wanted to involve your mother in this," Senior said, "but I had someone track you down at your last known residence, and learned you'd moved without a forwarding address."

"I see." She closed her eyes, trying to prepare herself for whatever came next.

"I've seen your credit report. I know how deeply in debt you are. And I saw photos of the apartment building, Valerie. I can't believe you were living there."

Horrified at the intrusion into her privacy, she almost couldn't answer. "We don't live there anymore. We're in a very nice place. I have a great job, with benefits. I was just down on my luck for a little while."

"Over a year. And you got fired for sexual harassment. Apparently you haven't changed. Still going after what you can't have."

Ice flowed through Valerie's veins. "What do you want?"

"To see you."

"Why?"

"I'll explain it, but in person."

"Well, I have no interest in that. At all. Goodbye." Anger like she'd rarely known surged through her. She hung up, then ignored the immediate call back. She knew what he wanted. Now that Wagner was dead, Senior wanted to make sure that Valerie wouldn't sue the estate, wouldn't make public—or even to threaten it—how Wagner has messed up and had a child out of wedlock. Well, Valerie had promised long ago. No further action required. How dare he question her integrity like that?

Or maybe he wanted to offer her some cash to continue to keep quiet. That wasn't acceptable, either—or even desired.

Valerie shoved herself out of the chair, tossing the phone into the cushions, furious that he was intruding in her life again. He'd actually seen where she lived. He'd gotten a copy of her credit report. Nausea rose again at the thought. She shouldn't have forgotten his pull and power.

"Valerie?" David's voice came from the intercom, startling her.

She forced herself to move across the room and press the button to answer him. "Yes?"

A pause, then, "Are you okay?"

She swallowed, trying to settle her nerves. "I'm fine."

Another pause. "Okay. I need you here, please."

She didn't want him to see her yet. She needed a few minutes to calm down. "Will ten minutes be all right?"

His pauses seemed to have great significance, but she wasn't sure why. "Sure," he finally answered.

"Thanks." She knew she sounded too cheerful, too upbeat, but it was all she could manage. After a moment she sank into the sofa, fighting tears, but mostly fighting panic. Wagner Rawling, Sr., was a powerful man. He could make a lot of trouble for her.

She sprang off the sofa and headed for her locked documents box to dig out the contract she'd signed years ago but hadn't looked at since. A knock on her door stopped her in her tracks.

"Valerie?" David called out.

She swallowed a groan of frustration. "What?"

"Open up."

"I said I'd be there in ten minutes. You can't wait that long?"

"Open the door, Valerie."

She didn't have to obey his order, but she figured he might break it down, so she forced a smile and pulled the door open.

"What's wrong?" He came inside, took her by the arms.

"I— Nothing."

"Something. It's clear as a bell in your voice. Not to mention the look on your face when your cell rang earlier." His hands tightened. "How can I help?"

Her knight in shining armor. She almost gave in to his offer. It had been so long since she'd let anyone help her. She knew it was a fault of hers, but it was better to admit and accept it than to start allowing herself to feel complacent, to think that someone would always come to her aid. She knew how things worked in real life, especially with the class differences between her and David. She'd grown up with it.

Paid for it.

Just hold me. The need overwhelmed her but instead she said, "You can't," careful not to deny there was a problem, since he'd already recognized the existence of one.

"You're more than just my employee," he said quietly. "Let me help."

She stared at him, debating, tempted. "I'll be fine. It won't affect my work."

His jaw hardened. So. She'd made him angry, after all. She couldn't do anything differently, couldn't appease him.

"I'll come to the house in a few minutes," she said.

He moved his hands to her face. She watched him lower his head toward her. She could have stopped him with little effort, but she let him continue, let him kiss her. Then kissed him back.

His mouth was warm, his lips sure. His arms slid down around her, pulling her closer. She let herself enjoy him, ignoring her logical mind screaming at her to stop. No. She wouldn't stop. Couldn't. She needed him, if just for the moment.

He groaned into her mouth, spurring her to grab him and hold tighter. He molded his hands over her rear, tugging her against him. She gasped, tipped back her head. He dragged his mouth down her neck, leaving a damp trail with his tongue, setting her on fire, a wild, uncontained, uncontrollable fire.

She felt herself being moved backward—toward her bedroom. Reality came back into focus with a hard click of the lens—her conscience sharpening the view again, knocking down the fantasy.

"I can't," she whispered, frantic. "Please. I can't."

"And you won't let me help you?"

"There's nothing—"

Her cell phone rang. She moved away from him, grabbed it, looked at the screen, flipped it open. "Hey, Dixie," she said with relief, turning her back on David.

A few seconds later she heard the front door shut.

* * *

David headed straight for the garage. He took the Falcon and drove north, not knowing where he was going until the got there. By the time he'd parked and gotten out of the car, Gideon had come onto his deck to greet him.

"You alone?" David asked as he climbed the stairs, his muscles taut so that he moved stiffly.

"Yep. Want some coffee?"

His stomach rebelled at the thought. "No, thanks."

"Whiskey?"

David laughed a little. "I guess I look like I need it."

Gid nodded. "Woman trouble or Noah?"

"Both."

"Pull up a chair."

The last-day-of-September weather was perfect for sitting on a tree-shaded deck and talking. David hardly knew where to start.

"Things tense with your new assistant?" Gideon asked, getting to the heart of the matter, as he usually did.

"How'd you know this wasn't about Laura?"

"No sparks anymore. On her side, yes, in a desperate kind of way. But not yours. You only had eyes for the subtly sexy Valerie."

Since David hadn't even known how attracted he was to Valerie a month ago, he didn't see how Gid could've seen it, but he had a knack for noticing such things and seeing the truth.

"Complicates things, having her working for you."

David looked up, following the adventures of two squirrels chasing each other. "Yeah."

"If it's any consolation, she feels the same about you."

"Against her will."

Gideon's silence brought David's head down, leveling his gaze on his older brother. "Nothing to say?"

"Are you looking for advice?"

"Usually I don't have to ask."

"Okay." Gideon rested his elbows on his thighs, leaning

forward. "Sounds like she's being a lot smarter than you are. She overheard our conversation at the party, you know, when we were talking about you never getting married. She's a home-and-hearth woman. Anyone can see that."

"How do you know she heard me?"

"I had a different vantage point from you. You also said she's the best employee you've had. Why are you messing with that?"

David picked up a fallen pinecone and tossed it over the railing. "Because she turns me on."

"Plenty of women have done that. Plenty more will."

"She's keeping a secret, one that has her scared."

Gid's brows raised. "Any idea what?"

"No. Her past catching up in some way, I think. But she hasn't shared anything about Hannah's father or why he isn't in the picture. There's a story there."

"Sounds like a good reason for you to back off."

"Yeah." His shoulders dropped. "I'm tired."

"That's why you're here. To figure out how to change that." Gideon stood. "I'm getting another cup of coffee. Sure you don't want something?"

David shook his head. Gideon left, then all David could hear were birds, the squirrels and a whisper of wind in the trees. Gid's house was even more isolated than David's, and much smaller. He'd chosen a different path in life. Maybe he'd been the smart one, after all, to get out of the family business.

"So," Gid said, returning. "What do you plan to do about it?"

"About Valerie?"

He cocked his head. "No. I think not having a plan about her is the best way to go. Let things happen. What do you plan to do about the job and The Enforcer?"

David grinned at the old nickname they had for Noah. "Stand up to him."

Gideon nodded. "How can I help you do that?"

"Well, I've been working on an idea I'd like to run by you...."

Chapter Thirteen

Valerie kept waiting for a shoe to drop. Two shoes, actually—David's and Senior's. She decided they were taking lessons from each other, keeping her in suspense, in limbo. On edge.

Senior's call a week ago hadn't yet yielded any surprises, unwelcome or otherwise. She assumed he hadn't tracked down her address—yet, anyway—and he'd stopped calling.

And David had been professional and amiable, but hadn't attempted to kiss her again. He was leaving town this morning, but this time to go to Los Angeles for preliminary discussions for his new project, still excluding Noah from the plans. Having learned how controlling Noah was, Valerie wondered if it was a good idea to keep him in the dark.

But that was David's decision to make.

"Did you find that folder?" David asked as she stood in his bedroom watching him pack a change of clothes in case he stayed overnight.

"I put it in your briefcase. I also updated the information on your laptop and stuck that in, too."

"Thanks." He zipped up the bag and set it on the floor, then looked at her.

It had been all she could do to keep her hands off him all week, yet he hadn't seemed to have the same problem. Which should make her happy...

"What did you tell Noah about the trip?" she asked. "In case he says something to me."

"That I had a solid lead for some stateside business."

"What kinds of objections do you think he would raise?"

"Noah isn't a visionary. He needs all the details in place when a project is presented to him. He also likes status quo. Routine. He's never been good with change."

"Must be hard, then, since he has four children. That's the definition of constant change."

"One would think." He grabbed his suitcase and headed for the door. "I'll call you when I get to L. A."

She didn't want him to go. He'd been home for eleven days. While he'd gone to the office frequently, he'd been home a lot, too. They'd done a complete overhaul of his computers, PDA and offices, both at the house and at work. She'd spent time with him in the Roseville office and had come to really like Mae, who ran the place.

David stopped in the doorway. "Thanks for all the extra effort you put in the past week. I haven't been this organized in...well, ever. The new filing system is great."

"You're welcome. I hope your trip is successful." She wanted to kiss him goodbye. How dumb would that be?

"Me, too." He hesitated a moment longer. "I'll stay in touch."

She could follow him downstairs and say goodbye at the kitchen door or even outside as he drove off, but she stayed put, afraid she might do something to let him know how she felt.

How she felt. She'd tried her best to avoid acknowledging her feelings for him, but they filled up her mind, night and day.

He's not the marrying kind, she reminded herself constantly. He doesn't want children. There could only be pain ahead for her if she let the relationship go any further, get any more personal. She would fall in love; he wouldn't. Then at some point another woman would take her place. How could she live with that? She wouldn't be able to revert to being only his employee again, so she would be out of a job.

No matter how many times that refrain rang in her head, it didn't stop her from feeling. Caring. Being aroused by being near him.

Valerie stepped onto his bedroom balcony and waved goodbye as he drove off. She returned to his unmade bed, reached for the pillows, then stretched out instead.

The doorbell rang. She hopped off the bed. No one rang the front doorbell. Everyone came to the kitchen door and knocked.

She hurried down the stairs, could see the top of someone's head through the square glass panes at the top of the door. Gray hair. A man's style.

Valerie slowed as the bell chimed again. *Senior.* He'd found her.

"I know you're in there, Valerie," he announced. "And I know you're alone. You don't have to be afraid of me. Please open the door."

You can do this. He holds no power anymore. You do.

The thought calmed her. She opened the door.

He looked old. Not just older. Old. And he wasn't sixty yet.

He smiled, trying to look benign, but all she could see was his overbearing dominance when he'd learned she was pregnant with his son's child.

"May I come in?"

She hesitated. She should take him to the cottage, but she didn't want him in her private space. So she stepped back, inviting him inside silently, then leading him to the living room.

"Beautiful home," he commented, setting his briefcase on the floor at his feet, then taking a seat.

She had no intention of signing whatever documents he'd brought along.

"David Falcon has a good reputation," he went on as she stayed silent. "Good head for business. Stays out of trouble."

She took a seat so that she put herself even with him, not the help waiting for orders. "Please get to your point."

"I understand that you don't want to see me. What I did years ago... I regret it more than I can tell you."

Too little, too late.

"Valerie, I want to get to know my grandchild."

Shock zapped her. In her wildest dreams she hadn't imagined that. Reputation was everything to him and his wife. How could they acknowledge a bastard child?

"No way," she finally said.

"Think about your daughter. She's entitled to know her grandparents, too."

"I do think about her. I put her first, always. And I've grown up a whole lot since you last badgered me into doing things your way. You don't wield that power anymore."

"I can see you have. And I hope you can see a man in pain, a man in mourning for his only child. You're a parent. Surely you understand what I'm going through. What Wagner's mother is going through."

Oh, he was good. Play the grieving parent card. "The last I knew, she wasn't aware of Hannah's existence," Valerie said.

"She still isn't. Not until you and I settle things. I don't want to get her hopes up."

Valerie sat up a little straighter. "How do you think she'll feel being grandmother to the same child as her housekeeper?"

He smiled slightly—or was it a grimace? "I know it's an odd situation, but I think her joy would outweigh the...unconventionality of the circumstances."

"In the beginning, perhaps. But you wouldn't be a good influence, and that's why I'm saying no. You spoiled Wagner, gave him everything, and expected nothing of him.

Then you bailed him out of a jam he should have faced himself—the fact he was going to have a child. You raised a shirker."

A long pause ensued, then, "He never knew."

She couldn't have heard him right. "What?"

"That letter he sent you, telling you he didn't love you, telling you he'd gotten engaged the year before? He didn't write it. I did. Or rather, I paid someone to forge his handwriting."

Valerie dug her fingers into the chair arms. "Get out," she said, the words scraping painfully along her throat. Wagner had never known about his own daughter? What would've happened had he known? How would their lives have been different?

"I'm willing to take whatever you throw at me, Valerie, to do whatever you want in order to make it up to you. But I want a relationship with my grandchild."

"You're delusional. Get...out." She pushed herself upright.

He stood, as well, reaching into his briefcase and pulling out a large envelope. "Just look this over, please. Give me that much. For Hannah's sake."

When she didn't take it, he left it on the chair then walked to the front door. She followed several feet behind, her legs unsteady, her vision blurred.

"I'm staying at the Red Rover Inn. I'm not leaving town until I hear from you."

She tried to picture the private-plane-flying, five-star-only hotel guest at the Red Rover Inn. "Don't hold your breath."

"You may change your mind when you see what's in the envelope." He opened the door.

"I can't be bought."

"Everyone has a price."

"Not me."

"Even you, Valerie. Because it isn't always about money."

The door closed with a click that echoed like a cannon blast in the entryway. Valerie didn't move for a long time. From where she stood she could see the envelope on the chair.

There would be money in it for sure, but what else? A new contract, replacing the old one—the one that she'd been coerced to sign when Senior told her Wagner was married. She should've sought legal help before she'd signed it, but she'd been too hurt and too angry, and without financial resources or even life experience to know what to do next. She'd signed it because she hadn't wanted Wagner to have rights to Hannah *ever.* He'd denied paternity. She didn't want him changing his mind later.

But the truth was that everything was based on a lie. Wagner had never known about Hannah.

Valerie had harbored such anger at Wagner all these years. But her anger should have been aimed at Senior and his lies.

She wouldn't make any more mistakes. This time she would know her rights and stand up to Senior.

First she had to see what he had in mind.

She grabbed the envelope and sat down, peeling it open, her hands shaking.

Valerie read a four-page legal document, then a one-page personal letter from Senior. Finally she stuffed everything back into the envelope and went out the back door and down the stairs to the cottage. Keep your head straight, she reminded herself. No emotions this time.

She got out a legal pad and started writing down her concerns and rebuttal points.

Then after staring at the phone for several long seconds, she picked it up.

"Thank you so much for seeing me so quickly," Valerie said to Laura Bannister as she took a seat opposite the attorney.

"You sounded pressed for time."

An understatement. Laura was probably being kind, because Valerie knew she sounded frantic. "The man I need to discuss is here in town. I don't want him hanging around longer than necessary, and he's not going away until I give him an answer—the answer he wants. If I don't do that, he may camp out here. Or make my life hell some other way."

Valerie launched into the details of her past and the predicament of her present and future, then shared the contents of Senior's envelope. Laura wrote notes and asked questions, then read the documents.

Valerie hadn't seen her since David said he'd broken things off with her. Going to a different lawyer would've been a wiser move for Valerie, if there'd been time. There hadn't been.

"The man writes a convincing, heartfelt letter," Laura said, putting aside the final piece of paper, a personal plea to Valerie from a father devastated by the loss of his son to the woman who'd loved that son once.

Valerie had fought tears while she read that letter. Senior's open emotion had swayed her in a different direction from the legal and financial document she'd first read.

"What are you wanting to hear, Valerie?" Laura asked, setting down her pen.

"Legally, can he force grandparent visitation, as the first document insists?"

"Probably so. The law is still broadening on the grandparents' rights issue, but unless you knew he would mistreat your daughter, it's doubtful he would be denied his right to know his granddaughter. You could drag it out in court for a while, but probably with the same results."

Valerie looked at her hands locked in her lap for a moment, letting Laura's words settle. "I figured that. I guess it comes down to the fact that I don't really want to deny Hannah the right to know her grandparents, not the other way around."

"I understand that. It's also very generous of you, considering what Mr. Rawling did to you. How he lied."

"I know he was horrified at the thought of his son marrying the housekeeper's daughter. I'm not excusing his behavior, but I understand it, especially now that I'm older and wiser and a parent myself. But I don't want any legal documents binding us. It should be a choice, one that Hannah is included in making."

"Very wise."

"Am I required to sign his documents?"

"No. If you fought him, he could pursue the issue in the courts and then you might have to sign agreements to appease a judge, but if you're willing to go along with what he wants, then there's no reason for documentation. Or the expense of a hearing."

"I'm not willing to do everything his way. He wants an official, carved-in-stone visitation schedule. I want to be flexible. And for a while, I want them to come here, until I know Hannah is comfortable being around them."

"That's reasonable."

Valerie looked around the office, gathering her thoughts, noticing the trophies and other beauty-pageant paraphernalia in a large glass case. "I don't want his money, at least not the check he included in the paperwork that covers my debts and then some. I incurred them, and I'm paying them off. The trust he wants to provide for Hannah's college education is okay, even a relief, frankly. I wouldn't turn it down. Her father would have provided that, if he'd known, I'm sure."

"Also wise. I know it's tempting to just turn down all offers, but you're being sensible to look at the future for your child."

"Well, I have to admit I like the idea of Hannah having a man in her life, someone she can count on," Valerie said. "My father left my mother and me when I was a baby. I know what it's like not to have male influence." It had driven her into Wagner's arms, desperate for love and attention. She'd known nothing about men then. Still didn't know much, to be honest. But she'd done some studying on the subject, since she was raising her daughter without a strong male role model, too, and she'd come to learn that not having one impacted a child for life. If she could get Senior to agree to her stipulations—

"Would you like to call Mr. Rawling and have him come

to my office?" Laura asked into the silence. "We could talk everything over together."

"Could I? Yes, thank you so much. That would be great. If only explaining it all to Hannah could be handled so easily."

"Does David know any of this?"

"No. It hasn't had any impact on my work."

Laura's brows raised. "I wasn't thinking professionally, but personally."

"He's my boss."

Laura hesitated, then set her clasped hands on her desk. "You know, Valerie, I didn't show up at David's house the day after the party to get your potato salad recipe."

The comment was so out of the blue that Valerie didn't respond for a minute. "After I heard you didn't cook, I realized that, but I never did figure out why you came."

"Really?" She smiled slightly. "David said goodbye to me for good that night. I wanted to check out the competition."

"Me? But—"

"Please don't insult me with denials. I'm not saying you were lovers. I'm saying your attraction to each other was so obvious to anyone looking more than a few seconds at each of you. Especially when you ignored each other all night. So, I had to check you out. Make sure you would be good for him."

"We're not lovers."

"Yet."

"A crucial point, however." She leaned toward Laura. "It's *my* problem. This time I need to be the one making the deals with Senior. Anyway, David's too protective. He might interfere."

"Protective? David?" She clamped her mouth shut, then apologized. "Believe me, he never acted protective of me. So, if you needed more proof…"

Valerie wasn't sure how she felt, that she seemed to need watching over while Laura apparently did not. "When should I ask Mr. Rawling to show up?"

"I'm booked until five."

Valerie would have to find someone to watch Hannah. "I'm sure he'll agree. If there's a problem I'll call you."

They both stood. Laura gestured toward a bag on her desk. "Thanks for bringing me lunch."

"Thanks for giving up your lunch hour for me—and for your honesty. I'll see you at five."

Valerie could have stopped by the Red Rover Inn, but she didn't want to tip her hand with Senior, so she called him from her car instead. Then she contacted Aggie and made arrangements to drop off Hannah later.

Having time to kill, Valerie sat in her car, wondering how to pass the two hours until Hannah's bus brought her home. David's house was spotless. The cottage, too. He'd left no Falcon work for her. She'd shopped for groceries two days ago. There wasn't enough time to go to a movie. Dixie was working.

Her cell rang. David.

"How's it going?" she asked.

"We're butting heads."

She could hear the smile in his voice. Apparently, he liked the negotiation aspect.

"I need you to research something in the company database, then e-mail it to me." He gave her the details.

"I'm about fifteen minutes away from the house," she said. "Will that be a problem?"

"I need it ASAP."

She started the engine. "I'm on my way."

"Thanks. Everything okay?"

"Yes. Why?"

"You sound…strained."

"Just in a hurry to get the info for you."

She'd come to understand that he went silent when he didn't believe her, as if waiting for her to correct herself and tell the truth.

"I don't like to talk on the cell phone and drive at the same time, David."

"Okay. Later."

She ended the call. As she drove she wondered whether Laura was right—that she should tell David what was happening.

No. She needed to do this on her own. She'd made a mess of it the first time around. She needed to do it right and be proud of herself, knowing she could make the right decisions and carry them out.

No knight in shining armor necessary.

Just the strong man inside it.

Chapter Fourteen

David struggled to keep close to the speed limit on his way to Chance City from the airport. He was always glad to get home, but never more so than today. It seemed as if he'd been gone a week rather than not even a full day.

He pulled into his garage then headed to the house, anxious to share the news with Valerie, but music blared from the cottage, so he changed direction and moved down that path.

The door was open, but he didn't see anyone. He knocked. When no one answered, he debated about stepping inside. On the one hand, it was private space. On the other hand, the door was open. Belle hopped off the sofa and came running.

He crouched to pet his dog just as Hannah whirled into the room, dancing in circles, her expression one of utter joy. She stumbled a little when she saw him, then grinned and made two more pirouettes. "Ta-da," she said.

He clapped and she bowed. Belle barked happily, joining in.

"I think you're supposed to curtsy," he said.

"What's that?"

"Men bow. Women curtsy." He started to show her then realized how ridiculous he would look—clumsy and awkward. "Ask your mom."

"Okay."

"Where is she?"

"At the big house. We ran out of ice cream."

"Have you started dance lessons yet?"

"I'm working on it. She says maybe in the spring."

"Did you tell her about…the other day?"

Her hackles went up a little. "No, but I did everything I promised. I haven't dusted your house again."

The music changed, and she began to sway to it. "Do you like to dance?" she asked.

"Kind of. I'm not very good at it."

"My mom's a really good dancer."

He knew she was, had danced with her at the Stompin' Grounds, but he couldn't tell Hannah that. He recalled holding her close, feeling her body along his….

He glanced at his watch. "You're up late for a school night."

"Just a little. Mr. Falcon?"

"You can call me David."

She shook her head. "Mom would shoot me."

"Is she a good shot?"

She giggled. "I don't think so."

"You had a question?"

"Do you think my mom is pretty?"

"Hannah!" Valerie stood in the doorway, a bowl of mint-chip ice cream in each hand.

Hannah's gaze dropped to the ground. David was relieved not to have to answer her question but also felt sorry for her. She was a cute kid, self-confident and happy, but her mother kept a tight rein on her, especially in front of him.

"Go to your room," Valerie said quietly.

Hannah eyed the bowls of ice cream that her mother set on the kitchen counter. "But I'm hungry."

Valerie said nothing. After a couple of seconds, Hannah turned around and ran to her bedroom, shutting the door hard. Belle followed, her claws clicking against the floor. She stood outside Hannah's door, looking back at David as if begging him to open it for her.

"I'm so sorry," Valerie said the moment her daughter was out of sight. "That was rude. I'll talk to her."

"She's very…high energy."

Valerie managed a laugh. "Nice way to put it. Do you want some ice cream?"

"No, that's okay."

She waved it in front of him. "It's your favorite."

"Okay, you talked me into it."

She passed him a bowl. "I'll go check on her and be right back." She picked up the other bowl and took a couple of steps, then turned around. "I didn't even ask how your meeting went. You're home a lot sooner than I expected."

"It's good news. I'll wait here for you." He ate the ice cream as he wandered through the space, noticing the personal touches she'd added that softened the look of the room, making it lived in, not like a hotel room as before. She'd put out family photographs, a few knickknacks and fresh flowers. There were colorful kitchen canisters and towels, and a ceramic bowl filled with fruit—grapes draped artfully over the edge, and a few apples and pears.

He sat on her sofa, finishing up the ice cream, feeling like a stranger in his own property, as if he were violating her privacy. They always met up at the house, spent the most time in his office together. This was…personal. Intimate.

Sort of like this morning as he'd packed for his potential overnight trip to L.A. He couldn't remember a previous time where she'd been in his bedroom at the same time he was. Seeing her standing there by his bed, her hands folded neatly in front of her, had been a challenge to his control. He wanted to know what those graceful hands would feel like against his skin, what her hair would look like spread out on his pillow. What her body looked like, period. He knew from observation that her breasts would just fill his hands, her waist and hips were narrow and her rear round and firm. She moved quietly, efficiently, elegantly. Class. She had a lot of class.

And she kissed like there was no tomorrow.

He wished she would loosen up, though. She didn't need to be so strict with her daughter or not let him help her out when she apparently needed help. Whatever secret she'd been keeping lately couldn't be so awful she couldn't share it with him, could it?

She came into the living room just as he finished the ice cream.

"Let's go up to the house and get you some," he said, standing.

"I'm fine. Really. Anyway, I'm anxious to hear what happened."

He saw lines on her face and a tight jaw. Something had happened since he'd left this morning. But she kept her secrets to herself, and he knew that asking her wouldn't do anything except put her on the defensive.

"Nope. I feel too guilty. Tell Hannah you'll be back in a few minutes."

She hesitated, her gaze locking with his, then she turned around. A few seconds later he heard voices from Hannah's bedroom, although no distinct words, then Valerie walked beside him to the house. Belle followed, reluctantly. She probably felt she needed to stay with the overwrought Hannah.

Well, he'd maneuvered that well, he thought with satisfaction. He'd get a little bit of time alone with her. "Peterson and Koning like the idea," he said as they walked. "They'll research all those issues that need researching in such a venture, then get back to me, probably within two to three weeks."

"At which point you'll take it to Noah?"

"Yeah. I'm seeing a light at the end of the overseas-travel tunnel."

"Would you give that up completely?"

"I hope so."

The night was cool. Mid-October now, they were well into autumn in the foothills, a time of warm days and cold nights. The leaves were turning gold and brown, with just a few red scattered here and there. Intermixed with the evergreens, it made for a beautiful palette, one he'd paid little attention to for the past few years, and yet one of the reasons he'd built his house where he had.

But then, he rarely had time for any of the things he used to enjoy—hiking, fishing, bike riding. He and Joe hadn't backpacked and camped in three years.

He was aware of Valerie next to him as they climbed the stairs. Never overly talkative, she seemed extraordinarily quiet now. And the strain on her face… And her short fuse with her daughter…

Yes, something had happened while he was gone today. Something major and emotional.

"Your mother called today," Valerie said as they entered the kitchen. "She said your cell was turned off."

"As you know, I don't turn it off. I saw it was her and let it go to voice mail." He opened the freezer and grabbed the carton of ice cream while she got out a bowl.

"She was curious about me," Valerie said.

"I imagine she was."

"You never talk about her."

He got the ice cream scoop from the drawer, took her bowl and served her. He could tell she was uncomfortable with him doing that for her, which, oddly, pleased him. "I rarely even think about her."

"Why?" She put a hand to her mouth. "I'm sorry. None of my business."

"No, it's fine, and no big secret." *Unlike yours.* "She and my father divorced when I was eleven. My father retained full custody, as he had with Noah and Gideon when he divorced their mothers. My mother didn't even demand regular visitation, so I didn't see her often, but particularly after she remarried and had two more children. Every so often she starts feeling maternal for one reason or another and she'll call."

Valerie leaned against the counter and took a bite of ice cream. "Where does she live?"

"Florida." He shoved the carton back into the freezer with undue force, then pushed his hands in his pockets and made himself relax.

"So, you grew up in an all-male household? Or did your father marry again after that?"

"Fortunately he stayed single. Then he died when I was eighteen."

"Was he a good father?"

David mulled the question over. "A good father. What would that be?"

"I don't know, since mine abandoned my mother and me when I was almost two. My experience with fathers is strictly vicarious—and fantasy, based on television fathers."

"Yeah. Reality sucks."

She laughed, as he'd hoped she would. "I don't know. I've seen some good ones out there. Hannah talks about her friend Gabby's father as if he were a saint."

David took advantage of the opening she'd given him. "You said Hannah's father is out of the picture?"

Valerie went very still, then she lowered her bowl. "Her father was never in her life, but he also recently passed away, so there will never be any hope of a relationship there."

"Did you want one?"

"For Hannah, yes, of course. He wasn't a bad guy."

"Doesn't sound like a gem to me."

"There's a lot more to the story. I just found out that he

hadn't known about her existence. So, a lot of the resentment I harbored for him wasn't warranted."

"Does that have something to do with what's been going on with you lately?"

Her mouth tightened. "Yes."

He waited for her to tell him what had happened today, but, as usual, she didn't open up. "So, you've forgiven him?"

She frowned. "I hadn't thought about it, because— Well, I guess so. Mostly I feel sad that he never met her. That he never got to see what a great kid she is."

"You've been her sole support all this time?"

"Yes." A light tone, matter-of-fact. She scooped out another bite.

David watched her eat the ice cream. As soon as she swallowed, he took the bowl and spoon from her and set them aside, his gaze never leaving hers. Then he leaned in and kissed her, as he'd been wanting to since the last time, over a week ago. Her mouth was cold and tasted of mint and chocolate. She warmed quickly, both her mouth and her reaction. She wrapped her arms around his neck, pulling herself close, groaning.

It was all the permission he needed. He sought the inside of her mouth with his tongue, slid his hands down her body over her rear, drawing her even closer. She grabbed his hair between her fingers, then dragged her hands down to frame his face, all the time coming at him full force, kissing him, enticing him.

He lifted his head and looked into her eyes as he slid a hand over her breast, feeling her nipple, hard against his palm, hearing her sigh, her eyes fluttering shut.

"This is so wrong," she whispered.

"Feels right to me. Perfect, in fact." He covered both breasts, filling his palms, then he pressed his lips to her jaw and slid along it to her ear, nosing her hair out of the way. She smelled incredible, tempting. Apricots? Hot, anyway. He moved in for more.

But she pushed away after a minute, tunneled her fingers through her hair and looked straight at him. She put a hand against his lips, not letting him try to convince her to continue.

"I have to go," she said finally. "Hannah…"

One step at a time, he thought. "Speaking of Hannah, I've learned she'd really like to take ballet lessons."

Her change of mood was instantaneous. "How do you know that?"

He measured his response. "She told me."

"And in what conversation could a subject like that just happen to come up?"

He ignored the question. "I'd like to see her go for it. I'll pay for the lessons."

"If and when I determine she should have them," she said, crossing her arms, "I'll pay for them."

"You're angry that I'm offering?" he said, surprised. He'd thought she would be pleased. He knew Hannah would be. "Every kid deserves to go for their dream."

"She's not your kid, and I'm your employee," she said, closing her eyes. When she opened them she was calmer. "I know I've broken rules here with you, but Hannah has to stay out of anything having to do with you."

"Wait a minute. That sounds like you don't trust me."

"I'm talking about emotions, David. I don't want her getting close to you. Of course I trust you. If I didn't, we'd be gone." She walked away. "Good night."

After the door shut he wandered to the window to watch her until she got inside the cottage. Belle came up beside him, her tail wagging slowly. He crouched down and scratched her ears. "Well, that didn't go well, did it, girl?"

The dog closed her eyes, enjoying the affection.

"I should leave her alone, like I had been. I just can't seem to stop myself. So, maybe you can tell me what happened to Valerie today? Or are you siding with her—the sisterhood code or something?"

Belle whimpered.

"I thought so." He stood and headed toward the staircase. "Come on, girl. Let's go to bed."

But bed didn't help. He was too wound up—from his meeting with Peterson and Koning *and* from kissing Valerie.

She was right. It was a mistake to pursue any kind of relationship other than professional. He knew that. He didn't want to lose the best thing that had ever happened—

He blew out a breath. Yeah. His life ran smoothly now, thanks to her. His world was organized. His stress level was way down. Gideon had said that things would work themselves out with Valerie, but David wasn't sure he was right. Usually, having a plan in mind was a wiser course of action, something to focus on.

He hadn't planned to kiss Valerie tonight. She'd just been standing there eating ice cream, and he'd needed to kiss her. Maybe it was the strain and stress he saw in her eyes, maybe because she'd taken his away, he'd needed to do that for her, too.

He laughed at himself. "Right. That's why you kissed her. You just wanted to help. Because you've always been known for your charitable efforts."

The thought gave him pause. In the past he'd dated women who were strong, independent and self-sufficient. Not that that didn't describe Valerie, but she was different. There was something about her that made him wish she was a little less self-sufficient.

Well, how insulting could he get? He could hear her reaction to that idea, could see her eyes narrow and her mouth tighten.

He really needed to figure out why he wanted so much to take care of her.

Chapter Fifteen

"We agree to your terms," Senior said to Valerie on the phone the next morning. "When can we meet Hannah?"

"All my terms?" she asked, dropping onto her sofa. "You will visit her here, with me in attendance, until I feel she's okay to be alone with you?"

"Yes."

"You won't pay any of my debts, even anonymously?"

"I won't."

She wasn't sure she could believe him, but she had to start somewhere.

"Have you forgiven me for keeping her a secret from Wagner?" Senior asked, his voice steady.

"I'm working on it, for Hannah's sake. The harm you caused by not telling Wagner is one you have to live with, the fact he died without knowing her. And Hannah may never forgive you for it, either, you know."

"Will you tell her now, before we even meet?"

"No. I'll let her get to know you. I decided she's too young for that burden."

"Thank you for that. So. When can we see her?"

"I'll talk to her today when she gets home from school. I'll call you afterward with her reaction. The decision to meet you is hers, as we discussed."

"All right. I'll be waiting to hear from you, then. Goodbye, Valerie. And thank you."

Valerie needed to call Laura and let her know. The negotiations that took place in her office were successful because of Laura's efforts. She'd asked Valerie what she wanted, then went about accomplishing it all for her, telling her to keep quiet unless Laura directed a question at her. Valerie hadn't been anywhere near as nervous as she would've been otherwise. She knew she had the upper hand this time.

She finally felt all grown-up.

So why was she so wound up now?

She looked at the phone, knowing she needed to make another call. She dialed the familiar number.

"Hi, Mom. Got a minute?" Her heart pounded harder than it had with Senior, roaring in her ears and chest.

"Sure. The Rawlings have gone back to L. A. What's up?"

"Well, it's about the Rawlings, actually. Senior paid me a visit yesterday."

"Why?" Panic coated the word.

"He and Mrs. Rawling want to meet Hannah."

"I knew I shouldn't have given him your number. I knew it. I wasn't thinking fast enough. You said no, of course."

"Mom, as you pointed out, he would've found me, whether or not you gave him my number. And, no, I didn't say no to him." She explained how everything had come about. Her mother said nothing. She didn't interrupt, didn't ask a question. "What are you thinking?" Valerie asked into the ensuing silence.

"That it's a big mistake."

"Why?"

"He's already proven to be a liar by not telling Wagne about your being pregnant. What makes you think he'll abide by the rules you're setting up?"

"He has too much to lose if he doesn't."

"You know I'm going to lose my job because of it."

Valerie frowned. "Why would you?"

"Because the missus will want to put distance between us She won't like us both being Hannah's grandmas."

"Well, maybe you should beat her to the punch and get yourself another job. You've been threatening to do that for years. I know you've had offers."

"Oh, well, there's a great solution. Me change my life completely so that it's easier for you. Honestly, Valerie, you are so selfish. All you care about is yourself."

Stunned, Valerie clutched the phone. "How can you say that? That's not true at all."

"You got pregnant, even after I gave you the birth-control speech. You accepted money from Senior so that your life would be easy instead of making your own way and paying for your own mistakes, like I did. You moved far away from me, even though it meant I wouldn't see you or my grand-daughter very often."

"You made me move out, Mom! You said I couldn't stay in the house, where Mrs. Rawling might see that I was pregnant. Mr. Rawling sent me to business school so that I would have skills to support myself, otherwise I would've gone on welfare. Would you have been proud of me then? I've made my own way since then. Completely. We've never been without food and shelter, even if it wasn't the best. And all without any help from anyone, including you. And it's never seemed to matter whether or not you see me or Hannah, or even talk to us. Now that you'll be in competition with Mrs. Rawling, maybe we'll hear from you more."

The silence that followed was the loudest Valerie had ever heard. She'd gone too far. Way too far.

The line clicked, then a dial tone followed, loud and accusing.

Valerie's chest heaved. She buried her face in her hands. It was all too much. First finding out that Wagner was dead, then that he'd never known Hannah existed, then Senior tracking her down, making demands. She'd countered them well, was proud of herself for that, but it was still stressful. And she had to tell Hannah today about her grandparents.

And now her mother. And her own words that would haunt her forever.

Secrets. It all came back to keeping secrets. If she'd been able to confide in her mother instead of having a secret relationship with Wagner, maybe that would've turned out differently. Oh, she wouldn't have wanted to be without Hannah for anything, but maybe there would've been a better resolution.

Then there was Senior keeping Hannah a secret from Wagner.

Secrets hurt. Crushed. Destroyed.

Now David—confusing, tantalizing, sexy David, who'd lit a fire under her, sparking flames where none had flared for a long time. Her feelings for him were a secret.

She wanted to run away from it all.

She couldn't. She had a job to do. A child to raise. Bills to pay. Her plan to create a new life for herself hadn't materialized beyond her new friendship with Dixie.

She'd also resisted meeting men and dating, and she knew exactly why.

Valerie shook out her hands, trying not to cry. She pushed herself up and paced, then headed for the door, unable to calm down. She would get to work, do physical labor today, anything that involved effort, like vacuuming. Maybe she would clean up dead leaves in the yard, even though it was Joseph's job.

David had left at the same time as Hannah left for school, an hour ago, but on his mountain bike. The last time he'd taken a ride, he'd been gone for hours. She had time to really push herself cleaning.

She almost ran to the house, trying to keep her mind a blank. She hurried through the kitchen, up the staircase and down the hall into David's bedroom. His bed was ever messier than usual, the bedding jumbled and twisted, as if he'c had a sleepless night. She pulled everything off the foot of the bed, leaned over to straighten the bottom sheet.

A noise intruded. She turned around. David stood there naked except for a towel knotted at his hips, his hair wet.

"When did you get back?" she asked, when she should've apologized and excused herself. She wasn't herself at the moment. She was Valerie, but not a person she recognized She was wound tight, in need of a way to relax and forget

"Long enough ago to take a shower," he said. "I pulled a muscle—or something—in my calf." He moved closer, limp-ing a little. "What's wrong?"

She didn't want to talk about it. Didn't want to think about it. She reached out and touched her fingertips to his chest, warm and still damp.

"Valerie," he said, soft and rough at the same time.

Paralyzed with indecision, she met his gaze. She didn't know what he would see in her eyes, but in his she saw curi-osity give way to desire. She didn't want to think anymore.

"Are you sure?" he asked, flattening her hand against his skin.

"No."

He smiled, sort of. He slipped his arms around her and brought her next to him. "Scared?"

"Excited. Needy." It had been building for a long time, too long, without resolution…or satisfaction.

He touched his forehead to hers. She felt his breath, warm and a little shaky, against her skin. She trembled at his tenderness.

"I want you," he said.

She wanted him, too, but couldn't form the words, so she just nodded.

He didn't waste another second. His mouth was on hers in

a flash, hot and searching. She ran her hands over his bare torso, savoring the freedom to touch him.

"You're beautiful," she said against his mouth.

He smiled. "That's my line."

"I'm not—"

He kissed her, stopping the words, scattering rational thought. He moved her toward the bed. When her legs touched it, he unbuttoned her blouse and tossed it aside. She wasn't wearing any lacy, pretty lingerie, not having anticipated such a thing happening, not owning any, regardless.

He nuzzled her neck as he unhooked her bra and let it fall to the floor. She felt it land on her feet, then a second later his hands were covering her breasts, his thumbs circling her nipples, then rubbing, teasing.

Her head dropped back.

"I knew you'd look like this," he said. "Feel like this." He moved down until he took a nipple in his mouth. "Taste like this."

Arching her back, she wrapped her arms around his head and groaned as he shifted to the other nipple. She felt his fingers slip under her waistband. The button popped open, the zipper slid down. One tug and her pants joined her bra on her feet, then he slid his hands under her panties, over her rear and squeezed. He pushed her underwear down, knelt before her to slip them and her pants over her feet. Then she was naked....

And vulnerable.

"I'm not on the Pill," she said, reaching for his towel as he stood.

He spread his arms, giving her permission with the gesture. "I'll take care of it."

Then he was naked, too, in all his exquisite glory, his beautiful swimmer's body lean and muscled, his erection flattering and tempting. She touched him, tentative for only a moment, then wrapped her hand around him, feeling him surge in her palm, hearing him release a long, low sound of appreciation and need.

He kissed her, hard and intense, changing angles again and again, demanding and bestowing, offering and taking. She'd never felt so…necessary to someone. So desired. She found freedom in his need, home in his touch. She realized her previous resistance to him had little to do with her sense of independence or even being in his employ. She'd been resisting loving him, something that had been happening slowly, steadily, since the day she'd come to work for him.

I love you. She said the words in her mind as he urged her to stretch out on the bed then lay beside her, setting his fingers at the base of her throat, then dragging his hand down her body, between her breasts, barely brushing the sides, along her stomach, across her abdomen, stopping where her thighs met. She squirmed. He took his time exploring. She opened to him, clamped her mouth before she begged him out loud, then let out a husky cry as he slipped a finger inside her. His thumb moved, too. Her hips rose. She called out his name.

"That's it, baby," he whispered. "Let it happen."

She had no choice. It was happening with or without effort on her part. He knew where to touch, where to tease, when to move, when to stop. Then when he put his mouth on her intimately, passionately, she took everything he gave. He didn't give her a moment to float back into consciousness before he was on top of her and in her and moving, filling her up, taking her high again, higher still, peaking at the same moment as he, lost in him.

I love you. Again the words came, silent and devastating. Why did she fall in love with men she couldn't have?

He sprawled on her for a while, his weight on his elbows, then rolled to his side, taking her with him, keeping her close. "I guess that had built up a while in both of us," he said.

She ran a finger around his chest. "How long for you?"

"Since I saw you in your bathing suit that first day." He toyed with her hair, sifting through it with his fingers, rubbing the ends. "How about you?"

"I don't know exactly. A long time."

He pulled her head back and kissed her, a leisurely exploration.

"Don't you have to get to the office?" she asked, feeling awkward suddenly, her problems seeping back into her thoughts, no matter how hard she tried to ignore them. Plus, he wasn't saying the right words....

"I may work from home today." He brushed his lips over her hair. "I'm not done here yet. How about you?"

She wanted to stay in his arms forever. "My boss is flexible."

He laughed quietly. Then he just held her, and she closed her eyes and let herself enjoy it.

"What's been bothering you?" he asked finally, his breath warm against her hair.

She felt her contentment die. "I don't want to talk about it while I'm naked and in your arms."

"But you'll tell me?"

"Yes," she said, making the decision. "Just not today."

He didn't say anything, but she figured he was annoyed. "I don't need to be taken care of, David."

"I figured that out."

She wanted to lean on him, though, wished she could have some burdens lifted. But she owed a lot of money, and just as she wouldn't let Senior clear her debts, she wouldn't let David, who would probably want to, as well. She'd considered asking him for a loan, with payments to come out of her paycheck at a lesser rate of interest than what she'd been paying, but had decided against that, too. And especially not now. They'd already mixed business and pleasure. There were bound to be repercussions for that.

"I want to help," he said.

"I know. And I appreciate it." She remembered Laura's reaction when Valerie had commented on David's protectiveness, how shocked she'd been. Maybe it *was* different for him this time. Maybe she meant more to him—

She couldn't think like that. She also didn't know what she was going to do now. What would their relationship be? Would he expect her to be available to him all the time now? Was their relationship exclusive or would he still date other women?

The phone rang. Valerie jumped at the intrusion. David didn't answer it, just letting it go to the machine. It was Noah.

"So, you're not answering your cell, and you're not home, either. This is getting old, David." He blew out a breath. "Okay, listen. Someone's been checking on our financial status. I need you in the office to work on this. Now." He hung up.

"That would be Peterson and Koning," David said. "Guess maybe I can't wait any longer to bring Noah in on the deal. I'd hoped—" He turned so that they were face-to-face. "I don't think I can ignore him now."

Valerie wanted him to go, anyway. She needed time to think about what came next. "I understand."

"I really don't want to get out of bed."

She smiled but said nothing.

He brushed her hair from her face. "I think you're glad to see me go."

She pressed her lips to his. "It was wonderful."

He ran his fingers along her jaw. "You're a complicated woman. When I hired you, I thought you straightforward and easy to figure out. You're not. There's a lot there."

"Good."

He kissed her long and lingeringly. She melted into him. Then he rolled off the bed and headed toward the bathroom. At the last second he turned around, catching her watching and admiring him.

"Should I call Noah and tell him you're on your way?" she asked, sitting up and pulling a pillow in front of her.

He smiled knowingly as she tried to hide her nakedness. "Too late, you know. I looked. And liked it all."

She stared back.

"Yes, that's a good idea to call him. Thanks." He disappeared around the corner.

Valerie grabbed her clothes and yanked them on, then sat on the bed to call Noah. David returned, dressed for work, as she hung up.

"He's…peeved at you," she said.

"He's about to become more peeved when he finds out I've kept him out of the loop on this project."

"Good luck," she said, not standing, not intending to walk downstairs with him and see him off, not wanting that awkward moment of whether to kiss goodbye or not. "Everything you need is on your desk."

He cocked his head. "Not going to kiss me goodbye?"

"What do you call what we did—" She pointed to the bed.

"That was hello."

Oh. So, she was being put on notice that this was just the beginning. "I know we should probably talk about this," she began.

He shook his head. "Why don't we just go with it, and see where it leads us."

"I wish it was that simple," she said. "I work for you."

"It doesn't have to get complicated, Valerie."

He was wrong about that, but there wasn't time to discuss it. "Right."

"I'll call you when I know about dinner," he said, then slipped an arm around her waist, pulled her up and kissed her until she kissed him back…and then some.

"We have to be careful," she said against his mouth. "Hannah—"

"I know. We will." Then he was gone, and she was left with regret mixed with exhilaration, satisfaction mixed with a brand-new kind of need. It didn't matter what spin she put on what had happened. Ultimately it came down to the fact that they were two healthy people who were attracted and did something about it.

Except that she was in love. And he wasn't.

Chapter Sixteen

"We can't lose," David said to Noah later in his office. "We're assuming some financial responsibility, but we have the potential to bring in a bundle."

"A loss is a loss, even when limited." Noah had gone from outrage at David's secret meetings, to stonewalling by coming up with hurdles to the success of the venture. "We have a reputation," he added.

"Not in Le Mans. In fact, it'll bring brand-new exposure to us."

"We've always been known for class and style. We cater to a limited clientele because of that."

"'Limited' being the key word. It's a new world, Noah. We need to grow and expand in order to stay competitive, but in ways that protect the company and our futures. We can't count on the sultan of Tumari forever."

"But you're talking about building race cars," Noah said. "That's risky."

"So was our business in general until recently. We're well established now. We've got a good name, a solid name, but no big name recognition. This will boost our recognition enormously. People will be talking about Falcon Motorcars. We'll get publicity like you wouldn't believe, much of it free."

"After investing millions."

"I've spent a lot of time and energy figuring this out, Noah. Then I talked to people who *do* know what will work. They think we've got a winner." David handed him a folder. "Here's your proof. The American Le Mans fan's demographics are perfect, and completely in alignment with our current buyer—the affluent 25- to 49-year-old with annual earnings well above the average. That's our market, especially for U.S. sales. We've been missing the boat there. Here's our chance to capitalize."

Noah pushed himself out of his chair and came to sit beside David on the office sofa. "I didn't understand how unhappy you've been with your job. I didn't believe Gideon when he said it."

"I can't keep up the pace, Noah. It's not like I'm quitting or anything, but I do want to oversee this branch of the company. It's my baby, my concept. Everything." David saw that Noah had calmed down. "We'll probably end up opening dealerships, because that fan will expect to walk into a showroom to buy a car with the latest innovations and technologies, ones we developed on our Le Mans car. And he'll be taking it home not just for the bragging rights but because it'll be the most amazing ride of his life."

"We'll be fully involved in all the decisions, right? We've worked too hard at building Falcon Motorcars to tarnish our reputation. If we lost business—"

"We can't lose. I'm telling you, we can't. I remember the mess we inherited, too, you know. Dad had vision but no business sense. But we're smarter, Noah. We've proven that. And we can end up with a slew of new buyers, probably young and American, all those new millionaires out there, and take the business in a whole new direction. We can hire a sales rep or two for the European market. We'll have our name all over the place on the circuit and then on the cars themselves."

"Would you move?"

David tried to get a handle on Noah. When he got very quiet, like now, he was impossible to read. Gideon could, maybe, but no one else. "No. And I'm not dropping out of the day-to-day business, just shifting job responsibilities."

"You're excited about it."

"Yeah." David couldn't even add to that. He didn't have the words. And this morning he'd made love with Valerie. Sweet, sexy, secretive Valerie. Everything in his life was unsettled— in a good way.

David pulled another folder from his briefcase and passed it to his brother. "Potential reps for overseas. Even if the Le Mans deal doesn't work out, I want to hire someone. I'd focus more on growing U.S. business. It's out there."

Noah tossed it onto his desk. "When do you think you'll have an answer from Peterson and Koning?"

"By the end of next week, probably."

"Let me look over all the details, and I'll get back to you."

Noah hadn't flat-out rejected the idea, but David couldn't gauge at all how Noah felt. He'd never had a lot of give in him, but even less since his wife died. And he ran his household like his business.

David glanced at his watch. Almost three o'clock. If he left now, he could beat the commute traffic on Highway 80. He stood. "I'm going home."

Noah nodded. "You'll be in tomorrow?"

Tomorrow was Friday. Hannah would be in school, which would give him time alone with Valerie without worries about being caught. Then he remembered, too, that next week was Hannah's fall break at school, when there would be no pos- sibility at all of time alone. That clinched it.

"I doubt I'll be in tomorrow."

"I'm sure we'll need further discussion on this matter, David."

"Don't talk to me like Dad, okay? We're partners. I've busted my butt for this business. If I want to work at home for a day, I will." He left without waiting for Noah's response, then cooled off during the drive home. Although maybe "cooled off" wasn't exactly accurate, because the anticipation of seeing Valerie again definitely didn't have a cooling effect.

He pulled into his garage and headed for the house, then spotted Hannah sitting in a lounge chair by the pool, her legs drawn up, arms wrapped around them, head buried against her knees. He debated what to do. The fact she didn't acknowledge him made him think he should just keep going. The fact she was usually cheerful—overly cheerful—made him detour to where she sat.

He took the seat next to her. "Bad day?" he asked.

She nodded.

"Wanna talk about it?"

She mumbled something into her knees.

"I can't hear you." He almost put his hand on the back of her head in comfort, she seemed so dejected.

She lifted her head slightly. "I'm mad at my mom."

"Where is she?"

"In the cottage. On the phone. Talking to my *grandfather*."

It was the first David had heard about a grandfather. "That's bad?"

Hannah finally looked right at him. Dried tears streaked her cheeks. "He was a secret. And now I have to meet him. *And* a new grandmother."

Which must have something to do with what Valerie had been keeping to herself lately, a family drama she didn't want him to know about. "You don't want to meet them?"

"Everything was fine, you know?" she said, fresh tears welling up. "We like it here. We *love* it here," she said with more drama. "I have a grandma already. She's not lots of fun." Her voice had softened, as if Valerie might overhear. "What do I need more for?"

"Having grandparents doesn't mean your situation here is going to change. You'll still live here." At least he thought so. Hoped so. What if Valerie had told Hannah something different? What if he lost Valerie? She'd promised she would stay....

He didn't feel comfortable trying to advise Hannah when he didn't know exactly what the situation was. But he could tell her what he'd been through himself. "When I was growing up, people came in and out of my life all the time. Even my mother." He saw Hannah focus more intently on him.

"Your mom didn't live with you?"

"She moved out when I was eleven. I saw her now and then, but mostly I lived with my dad and two half brothers."

"At least you had them. I don't even have that. I want a baby brother *so bad*."

The passion in her voice made him want to smile, but he treated her wish seriously. "Then I hope you get one. In the meantime, you have grandparents. I didn't have any."

"None?"

"Nope. They all died before I was born."

"That's awful."

"I thought so, too. When will you meet yours?"

"In two days. On Saturday. Mr. Falcon? Will you be there, too?"

Her hopeful look made him wish he could be. "I don't think that'll be possible."

"But I'm scared. My mom said they're very important people. I don't know how to act."

"Give them a chance. And just be yourself. They'll love you right away."

"That's what Mom says." She wrinkled her nose as if not believing it.

"Okay, then. Two people have said it, so you know it's the truth."

"Thanks."

He finally did brush his hand down her hair. "You don't have to thank me. If you ever need anything at all, just ask. If it's within my power, I'll do it."

"Hannah." Valerie came up the path, her eyes flickering to David, questioning and welcoming at the same time. How did she manage that?

"I dusted his office," Hannah blurted out.

Valerie stopped. "What?"

"That's our secret. Mr. Falcon caught me dusting his office. He told me not to do it again, and I haven't. I promise."

David swallowed a smile. "Yes, she's kept her promise."

"He told me I should tell you, but I didn't. But now I know that secrets are bad. I'm never gonna keep a secret again." She flung herself at Valerie.

David got up, excusing himself and walking away, but hearing Hannah say, "Mr. Falcon says I should give my new grandparents a chance. So I will, Mom."

He couldn't hear Valerie's murmured response, but all seemed well.

And he'd had a hand in that.

The next morning Valerie dragged her feet about starting work, unsure of what to say to David. On the one hand, she was grateful for his advice to Hannah the day before, which had calmed her enough that Valerie could have a good conversation with her. On the other hand, now that he knew bits and pieces of the issue, she needed to tell him all of it so that he wouldn't guess incorrectly.

They'd just begun an intimate relationship. She didn't want to discuss the first love of her life—not yet—but now she had no choice.

A few minutes after Hannah boarded the bus, Valerie

finally worked up the nerve to climb the stairs to the big house. David was waiting. The moment she opened the door he swept her into his arms and kissed her.

"Good morning," she said, a little dazed and a lot aroused.

"The bus was three minutes late."

She laughed. He grabbed her hand and led her through the kitchen, then at the bottom of the staircase, he swept her into his arms and carried her up the stairs and into his bedroom. The romantic gesture thrilled her, emboldening her enough to take the lead and undress him. She tantalized him with her fingertips and her lips. He drew in air, the sound sharp, as she teased him. His fingers threaded her hair as she moved down his body, her need to touch and taste overwhelming. And his being naked while she was fully dressed seemed so much more…erotic? Intense? Definitely both of those.

But he didn't wait too long to get her just as naked, and then they landed on the bed and rolled, locked together. She loved the feel of his skin against hers from head to toe. Loved that he needed her so much but made the effort to drag out the experience so that when he finally entered her, she went into a climax instantly, arching to meet him, her head thrown back, long, low sounds coming from her.

The moment she ebbed he rolled so that she was on top. Her hair fell around her face as she rested her hands alongside his head on the pillow. He lifted up, caught a nipple in his mouth and gently pulled her lower, moving to the other side, then sliding his hands where his mouth had been and pushing her up again. His hands drifted to her hips, helping her move in erotic rhythm, until he found release, too. She loved watching him, was flattered by the absolute pleasure and satisfaction on his face.

Finally he dragged her down on top of him and held her. She settled against him, wishing it could go on and on, but reality reared its head again. She knew she had to tell him things about her life that she didn't want to bring into the relationship when it was so new and vulnerable.

David resituated her, pulling up the bedding against the chilly morning.

"So," he said. "You've been having some excitement lately."

"You could call it that." Maybe it was better this way—in bed, tucked close, where she didn't have to look at him.

"How about starting at the beginning?"

She closed her eyes for a moment, her hand pressed to his heart, which beat strong and steady. She'd gotten to know him well over the past two months, had fallen in love with him, foolishly or otherwise. Now she had to trust him more than ever.

"I told you my mother worked for a family in Palm Springs as their housekeeper."

"I remember."

"It's their vacation home, but they spend a lot of time there, often coming just for weekends, but weeks at a time, too. Wagner Rawling, Sr., whom everyone calls Senior, and his wife, Loretta, plus their son, Wagner Jr."

"I take it this story is about Junior."

"Yes, although he's called Wagner. We grew up together, sort of. He was four years older, but we'd known each other almost all our lives. As children, we played together a lot. My mother didn't like it, but the Rawlings didn't discourage it. When Wagner turned sixteen, his world expanded, and I no longer mattered to him.

"I missed him. I'd always looked forward to his visits, but he would ignore me, or worse, treated me like help. Then when I graduated from high school, he came home after finishing college and we discovered a different connection. We became lovers. I fell in love and got pregnant, but before I knew I was pregnant, he left for Europe for several months. He was supposed to return and work in the family business."

While she talked, David ran his hands over her back, soothing, making it easier to tell him everything.

"I didn't know how to get in touch with him, so I had to ask his father, who noticed the changes in my body and confronted me about it. I confessed I was pregnant. A few days later he gave me a letter from Wagner that said he'd never loved me, and had been, in fact, engaged to be married for a year. He'd apparently told his father I'd slept with several guys, and I was only looking for money."

"But?"

"He was my one and only. He'd done the seducing, and I fell as hard as any eighteen-year-old without life experience falls for a man who knows the ways of the world. His father made me a deal—he would pay all my expenses for having the baby, plus send me to business college."

"Where was your mother in all this?"

"Really angry at me for jeopardizing her job, but also telling me to take the deal, that it was more than I deserved."

David's body went taut. "More than you deserved? But—"

"Don't go there, okay?" She squeezed her eyes shut. "It's taken me years to forgive her for that. Anyway, while I was making up my mind about what to do, Wagner got married. That was the end for me. We had no contact at all, never once discussed the situation."

"DNA tests would prove paternity."

"Yes, but by then I didn't want him acknowledged as the father."

He hesitated. "You said he died."

"Recently, in a boating accident."

"And now his parents have materialized, wanting to know Hannah."

"Wagner and his wife didn't have other children. Hannah's the only tie to their son. But the worst thing is that Senior also confessed he'd written the letter, that he'd never told Wagner I was pregnant."

Valerie could feel David's outrage. His arms tightened around her.

"So, why the hell are you dealing with him?"

"Because of Hannah. They are her grandparents. Mrs.

Rawling, in particular, doesn't deserve to be shut out, since she wasn't involved. She's grieving for her only child. Hannah could help."

"You're much more generous than they deserve."

"Maybe. But when you're a parent, you think differently. Believe me, I'd like to deny them the right and keep her to myself, but I can't do that to her. You saw her yesterday. Think how she would feel if I didn't tell her, then she learned on her own later. It could cause years of estrangement and hurt between us. Better to deal with it now."

"How is—"

She put her hand against his mouth. "Shh. I don't want to talk about it anymore, okay? We won't have much time alone over the next week. Wouldn't you rather use this day to do other things?" She felt empowered suddenly. Self-confident.

And madly in love. *Mad* being the operative word. Foolish, too. One would think she would've learned her lesson about loving men she couldn't have.

But the heart wasn't so easily controlled.

So she gave him herself, everything she had to offer, and took back from him, whatever he could give, then slept in his arms for a while.

Regret could come later.

And undoubtedly would.

Chapter Seventeen

David made sure he was home when the Rawlings showed up on Saturday afternoon, in case of any fallout. He was standing on his deck when the well-dressed couple walked up the driveway, hand in hand. Mrs. Rawling seemed to be leaning on her husband, who carried a shopping bag in his other hand.

He watched the man give the woman an encouraging hug, then knock on the cottage door. The door swung open and the couple went inside. Valerie leaned out and spotted him. He lifted his hand in acknowledgment, then she disappeared.

He'd asked why she didn't schedule the meeting in a public location instead of in her personal space, and she'd said it would be easier on Hannah to be in her own environment. He supposed he saw the logic in that, but it would be easier to walk away from a restaurant than to get the Rawlings to leave her house, if things started to go wrong.

So David stayed where he was, just in case. After a few

minutes Joseph's truck came down the driveway. Grateful for a reason to get himself closer to the cottage, David went to greet his friend.

"Whose fancy Cadillac out front?" Joseph asked.

"Friends of Valerie. What's up?"

"You coming to the Stompin' Grounds tonight?"

"I hadn't planned on it. Why?"

"The Hombres are dropping in for a surprise visit."

"Surprise?"

Joseph grinned. "They want to try out some new stuff. We're trying to get a full house for them."

"It's been full every time I've been there, Joe."

"Sometimes it's slower than others. The Hombres want lots of feedback."

David shrugged. "I can't promise, but I'll try."

"Nine o'clock." Joseph headed back to his truck. "Don't be late."

"Hey, where're you going? You just got here."

"I figured a personal invite would get more people to come. I've got lots on my list," he said over his shoulder. "Maybe Valerie would like to come, too."

"I'll ask her, but I think she's going to be busy."

"Whatever. Dix'll probably call, anyway."

Then David was left waiting again and wondering. He should've talked Valerie into turning on the intercom and leaving it open for him to hear. That way if the Rawlings caused a problem, he would know.

He shoved his fingers through his hair. What the hell was he doing? He hadn't wanted to get close to her daughter, yet here he was, on guard in case either of them needed him. He'd already acknowledged the stupidity of getting involved with Valerie, but that hadn't stopped him from doing it—or wanting to continue.

He took a seat in a pool chair, watched the cottage door and waited. They didn't emerge for hours. And when they did, he couldn't read anyone's expression.

* * *

Valerie spotted David sitting by the pool when they all came out of the cottage. She wondered how long he'd been there. The whole four hours since the Rawlings had arrived?

How could Laura have thought he wasn't protective?

He walked up to them, introducing himself before Valerie got the chance. She saw him exchange a look with Hannah, who gave him an unobtrusive thumbs-up sign, drawing a small smile from him. Their silent connection and communication gave Valerie pause. Somehow David and Hannah had gotten close. She wasn't sure when or how that had happened—nor how she felt about it.

"Hannah's grandparents are taking her out to dinner and a movie," Valerie said, as upbeat as possible. Valerie had left the decision to accept the invitation to Hannah.

"And I can stay up late." Hannah looked comfortable going with her grandparents.

"We'll have her back by ten-thirty," Senior said.

Valerie decided not to walk to the car with them, not wanting to hover. She kissed her daughter goodbye and watched her leave.

"It went okay, I gather," David said a minute later.

"Yes. They brought some albums with pictures of Wagner growing up. Hannah was fascinated. It was a smart thing to do. Opened her up to them right away. They told stories I hadn't known about, of course, too." She rubbed her arms. "I don't know how I'm going to stand the wait until she's home."

"I have an idea."

She focused on him. "I'm really not in the mood, David."

He laughed. "Not that, although that would be a good way to pass the time, I think, and make you forget for a little while. No, something else. Joe stopped by to say that the Hombres are playing at the Stompin' Grounds tonight, and they want a full house for them. They're trying out new material. So, how about going with me?"

"I need to stay by my phone."

"Put your cell on vibrate and stick it in your pocket where you'll feel it. We're only five minutes from home."

"But we don't want people to know we have a relationship other than business."

"We won't slow dance. Come on. It'll keep you busy. We'll go early and have some burgers. I'll have you back by ten. Plenty of time."

She really liked the idea of having a distraction. "Okay. Thanks. In the meantime, I need to keep busy. I think the kitchen cabinets need to be rearranged."

He smiled. "I'll be in my office, if you need anything."

"You don't want to help?"

"I wouldn't be able to keep my hands off you."

Valerie smiled back.

At the Stompin' Grounds, David was trying hard to respect Valerie's need for him to keep things from getting out of hand. They'd eaten dinner, had a beer and danced one fast dance, not touching at all. The Hombres were setting up. Valerie was hanging out with Dixie and her friends in their corner.

David leaned an elbow against the bar and sipped an icy beer, occasionally looking at Valerie as she laughed and talked with the other women. She fit in. He never would've thought he would say that about her. She'd seemed so reserved in the beginning, so solemn, but not any longer. She'd made a place for herself.

He took another swig, annoyed he couldn't slow dance with her, then spotted her pulling her cell phone from her pocket, looking at the screen as she headed outdoors to find quiet. He followed.

"How did you find out?" he heard her say as he caught up with her.

"I was waiting to tell you until I saw how it went," she went on. "I'm sorry you feel that way, but this is my life. My decision… I can't talk to you when you get like this."

David moved closer, letting her know he was there. She looked up, startled. "I'll call you tomorrow…. Okay, then, you call me when you're ready. Goodbye."

She tucked the phone into her pocket. "My mother. Mrs. Rawling called her to say how thrilled she was to be sharing a granddaughter. Mom thought she was gloating."

"Do you think that's true?"

"I don't know. I kept my distance from Mrs. Rawling while I grew up. She was very formal, and a demanding boss to my mother. But then, she grew up wealthy and entitled. My mother has never liked her."

"Why'd she stay on?"

"Security. And I'm sure the fact they weren't there full-time was also part of her decision. She threatened to leave every so often but never did anything about it. She's just not a happy person, David. I'm surprised Senior didn't find a reason to fire her after I got pregnant."

"He probably figured she would tell Mrs. Rawling about Hannah."

"Oh. I hadn't thought about that. So Mom's had the upper hand all these years and probably didn't realize it." Valerie shook her head. "Ah, irony. You've gotta love it."

From inside the bar came a voice announcing the Hombres and then music began to blare. "Would you rather go home?" David asked.

She shook her head. "I want to have some fun. Let's go dance."

By the time they got inside and squeezed through the crowd to where Joseph and Dixie were dancing, the song was ending. The lead guitarist took the microphone.

"Thanks for coming, everyone. We've got a new set we've been working on. We hope you like 'em all. Before we get goin' on the tunes, however, Joseph's got somethin' he wants to say. Joe?" He held out the mike as Joseph hopped onto the small stage.

He wiped his hands down his thighs, then reached for the mike. "You all know me," he said. It was followed by boisterous response, most of it insults, making him grin. "You all know Dixie." Cheers erupted.

Dixie raised both arms and smiled, but David was also close enough to see confusion in her eyes.

"We've been a twosome since before I could drive."

"Off and on," Dixie shouted.

"Mostly on. Now, I know you've put up with a lot from me Dixie Rae, and I'm hopin' you're gonna want to put up with a lot more." He pulled a small black box from his pocket and got down on one knee. Feedback on the mike screeched for a second, then quieted down. "I love you, girl. I'm asking you to marry me and have my babies."

Dixie's hands flew to her mouth, then she seemed to pull herself together, and used her hands as a megaphone to call out, "Well, what're you doing twenty feet away? Come put that ring on my finger, Joseph McCoy."

Amid cheers and whoops, Joseph did just that as the crowd separated, making a path for him to reach her. David caught a glimpse of Valerie, her eyes sparkling with tears, her fingers pressed to her lips. Tears of joy for Dixie? Something else? Valerie had a child, but no one had proposed marriage to her, as far as he knew.

But brave Valerie hugged Dixie then Joseph, then so did David.

"I'll want you to stand up with me," Joseph said.

"I'd be honored, Joe."

The band started playing again. Joseph and Dixie took the floor. To hell with not slow dancing in front of the others, David thought. He would ask Valerie to dance. But just as he was about to, she dug into her pocket for her cell phone and pushed her way outside. He trailed her.

"I'll be there in five minutes, Hannah, okay? Just sit in the chairs by the pool… I know it's cold. Five minutes."

Valerie turned toward the bar. "Oh! You're there. They're already at the house—more than an hour early! Can you drop me off, please?"

"Let's go."

A minute later in the car she said, "So were you surprised about Joseph proposing?"

"He hadn't said a word."

"Dixie looked so happy."

"She's been very patient."

"She loves him."

David looked at Valerie's face reflected in the dashboard lights, her expression calm, as usual. "Sometimes love isn't enough."

"Love conquers all," she said.

"No, it doesn't. Love changes. Love dies."

"Not true love. True love never dies."

She'd always been so practical and logical to him, that this particular fantasy about love seemed…unhealthy. "How do you tell the difference between true love and…any other kind?"

"You can tell."

They pulled into the driveway. He didn't know whether to be glad that the trip was over and the conversation was ending, or if the conversation should continue so that he could get her to see she was deluded to think love could last forever. It couldn't. He'd seen it fail too many times to believe that. It barely lasted beyond the honeymoon stage for most people.

"A while back you told me they were meant for each other," Valerie said serenely, quietly.

"I think if anyone can make it, Joe and Dixie can. After all, they've had fifteen years to figure it out. Generally people don't know each other a year before they make a lifetime commitment. No wonder relationships fail."

She patted his hand, a slight smile on her face, just as he came to a stop in front of the garage, deciding to park the car later. She pulled open the door and hurried up the path to the pool. Hannah met her halfway.

"Did you have a good time?" Valerie asked.

"I ate lobster!"

Valerie slid her arm around Hannah's waist and walked to where the Rawlings were waiting. "Did you like it?"

"It was good. And they bought me a bracelet. See?" She held out an arm, displaying a circle of sparkling pink gems.

Real? David wondered, coming up next to them.

"It's beautiful. You need to tell your grandparents goodnight."

David heard tension in Valerie's voice. Did Hannah?

"Good night," she said politely. "Thank you."

Mrs. Rawling hugged her, although Hannah kept her arms by her sides. "We'll see you tomorrow."

Hannah looked into Valerie's eyes then hurried off. Some kind of drama was happening, he decided.

Everyone stood silent until Hannah shut the cottage door.

"That bracelet is too expensive for a child," Valerie said.

"We have a right to buy our granddaughter gifts," Senior replied harshly.

Belle growled. Everyone turned toward her. David hadn't even known she was there.

"It's okay, girl," he said. "Go lie down."

She looked up at him as if she didn't want to obey, then moved a few feet away and sat, but didn't put her head down.

Valerie turned back to the Rawlings. "Children her age lose things. They don't understand the value."

Mrs. Rawling stepped in. "We impressed upon her that it was valuable and she should be careful with it."

"What's valuable to an eight-year-old—" She stopped, seemed to slow herself down. "Never mind. A bigger issue seems to be that you made plans to see Hannah tomorrow without talking to me first."

"Hannah brought it up, not us," Senior said, then looked at

his wife. "But Loretta and I did want to ask a favor. We understand Hannah has vacation from school next week. We'd like to take her to Lake Tahoe for a couple of days, if you don't mind."

Valerie crossed her arms. "Where would you stay?"

"We have friends who own a home there. They're not using it at the moment. I assure you we'll watch her every minute."

"I'll think about it. I'll call you in the morning and let you know my decision."

David admired her. She was holding her own with the couple, not seeming at all intimidated.

"We enjoyed our evening very much," Mrs. Rawling said. "She's quite a girl. High spirited, but sweet. I see a little of my son in her, in her eyes."

The woman's tone set David on edge, so he could only imagine Valerie's reaction. Hannah was a miniature of Valerie, including her eyes, both in shape and color.

"She's just Hannah," Valerie said. "My mother said you called her."

"I thought we should talk, yes." Her chin went up. Senior slipped an arm around her waist. "The situation is a little… awkward, don't you think? I was trying to make her feel at ease."

David would've ended the increasingly uncomfortable conversation right then, before it escalated, but it wasn't his place. Valerie would only accuse him of interfering. Fortunately Senior took charge.

"We need to go, my dear. Valerie, we'll be looking forward to your call in the morning."

The man was slick, David decided. He wished Gideon was there to take a better measure of him. But David knew for sure that Valerie needed to be careful of Senior and his power and pull. Should David warn her? Would she accept advice from him about it?

Probably not.

His option was to keep tabs. That much he could do.

Valerie didn't move until the Rawlings were out of sight, then she faced David. "I need to get inside and talk to Hannah."

"I know." He cupped her arm. "Are you going to let them take her to Tahoe?"

"I don't know yet. I don't trust them, David."

Okay. Good. She'd keyed in on it, too. He relaxed a little. "Trust your instincts," he said. "Good night."

For a moment, just a moment, he thought she was going to kiss him. She leaned toward him then suddenly turned away. He waited until she was inside before he climbed his stairs, Belle appearing from where she'd been banished to accompany him.

"You're worried, too, aren't you, girl?"

Belle barked once.

"We'll both stay alert, then. Between us, we can take care of them."

It was the last thing Valerie would want, to be taken care of. *Tough*. In this matter she had no choice. She'd been under his protection since the moment he hired her. And Hannah was part of the package.

He would protect his own.

Chapter Eighteen

For the second morning in a row, David awakened with Valerie in his arms, although she was still asleep this time. They'd slept late each morning since Hannah had gone to Tahoe. It had been an incredible couple of days, even with Valerie's tension never letting up. If anything, her stressed emotions had made her more passionate, more intense, more needy. They never spoke about what would happen next, how their working relationship would be impacted.

David's hope was that everything would continue as it was. Life was good. Perfect, in fact.

She stirred sleepily.

"Good morning," he said against her temple, this time smelling lemons in her hair.

"Morning." Her hand rested on his chest.

He covered her hand with his. "Sleep well?"

"Yes. And Hannah comes home today."

"You've missed her."

"It's the first time we've been apart for more than a few hours. But I've had other things to occupy my mind." She tipped her head back and smiled at him. "She sounds fine on the phone. I just need to see for myself."

He was about to take her mind off it when the phone rang. He picked it up.

"David, this is Ron Peterson. Can you make a meeting today in my L. A. office?"

"Are we finalizing things, Ron?"

"It depends on how this meeting turns out."

"I'll check on flights and get back to you." He hung up and stared at the ceiling, his heart racing. "This is it."

"They okayed the deal?"

"I should have an answer today. Last meeting, I hope."

"Then *lots* more meetings," she added, a smile in her voice. "I'm happy for you."

He hugged her tight. "Your help was immeasurable."

"My pleasure. Now, do you need me to get an airline reservation for you?"

"Yeah, thanks. Let me call Noah first and see if he wants to go, too."

Valerie threw back the covers and got out of bed. He wasn't in such a hurry that he couldn't take a minute to admire her as she pulled on her robe, not blushing like the first time she was naked in front of him, but not trying to tease him, either.

Natural. He liked that about her.

"I'll start the coffee," she said.

He nodded then reached for the phone.

A couple hours later he set his garment bag and briefcase by the kitchen door. He would pick up Noah, who was taking his first trip since his wife had died. He'd agreed to it only because Valerie had said she would stay at Noah's that evening, giving his nanny time to drive to Sacramento for a class at the university she took twice a week. Valerie had just gone to the cottage to pack a few items. After the Rawlings dropped off Hannah, she and Valerie would head to Noah's.

The phone rang. He saw the number was Valerie's cell, which she'd given Hannah to use.

"Hey, kiddo, what's new?" he asked.

"Mr. Falcon," Hannah said in almost a whisper.

He pressed the phone to his ear. "What's wrong?"

"Is my mom there?"

"She's in the cottage. Do you want me to get her?"

"No. You said I could tell you if I needed something, remember?"

He squeezed the phone tighter. "I remember."

"I heard my grandparents talking when they didn't think I could hear them."

David's entire body went on alert. "Okay."

"They were talking about me, how I would stay with them a lot, like all summer and stuff. Maybe more."

David relaxed. "It's all right, Hannah. They can't make you do that unless you want to. And your mom wouldn't let them, either."

"But, Mr. Falcon, I also heard them say how Mom had beer on her breath that night you guys had to come home early. My grandfather said something about an unfitted mother. Do you know what that means?"

And so it began, David thought. He *knew* the Rawlings couldn't be trusted. Hell, even Belle had known that.

This needed to be stopped before it got started.

"Mr. Falcon?"

"Yes?"

"You can fix it, right?"

"I will fix it. I promise you."

"Will you tell my mom?"

"After I fix it."

"She's not gonna like that. I promised I wouldn't keep any more secrets."

"I know. But we don't want to upset her, okay? Let me check on things first. Can you do that? Just for one day, Hannah?"

"Oh, here they come. Bye."

The line went dead. David knew the Rawlings planned to drop off Hannah at the cottage then take their private plane home to L. A. The timing couldn't have been more perfect.

The kitchen door opened and Valerie came in, smiling, anticipating her daughter coming home, and also happy in a way he hadn't seen before. He didn't want to see her unhappy again. Or worried. Or scared.

He kissed her goodbye, a promise in the embrace to protect her. No one would burden her ever again.

"What's going on with you?" Valerie asked her daughter late that evening as she tucked her into bed in Noah's guest room. Hannah had acted strangely all day, clinging to Valerie's side, not wanting her out of sight.

Hannah pulled the blankets to her chin. Her eyes were wide and serious. "I can't tell you."

She'd never seen her daughter like this. "What do you mean you can't tell me? No secrets, Hannah, remember? Is it something to do with your grandparents?"

"I can't tell you, Mom. I told Mr. Falcon."

"Mr. Falcon?" Stunned didn't begin to describe Valerie's reaction. "Telling me what's bothering you is much more important than a promise to Mr. Falcon."

"It's my grandparents," she blurted. "They want to take me away from you."

"What?" Fury burst inside her, red-hot and instantaneous. "How do you know that?"

"I heard them talking. They thought I was asleep."

"And what does Mr. Falcon have to do with it?"

"I called him, and he said he would take care of it. I knew he could fix it. I knew it." She pulled the blankets even higher so that just her eyes were revealed. "He said we would tell you tomorrow, after he fixed it," she mumbled under the covers. "Don't be mad."

Valerie didn't want her to be afraid of telling the truth, ever. "Honey, it's okay. I promise, it's okay. You did the right thing by telling me."

"But I don't want Mr. Falcon to get in trouble, Mom. He's my…friend. You know? He's really nice to me. Like a—" She stopped for a moment. "Like a dad," she finished, almost whispering. "My dad."

No! When had her daughter started fantasizing about David being a father to her? How had Valerie missed that? The other day she'd realized they'd talked and were friendly, but more than that? Did David know how Hannah felt?

How could he get her hopes up like that? He didn't want a wife and family, he'd made that clear. It was one thing to have a relationship with an adult woman who knew what she was getting into, but a child?

"Everything will be okay, Hannah," she said to her worried-looking daughter. "Just go to sleep."

"You'll come sleep with me?"

They had to share the guest room, but Valerie wouldn't go to bed until the nanny, Jessica, got home from Sacramento.

"Yes, I'll sleep here." Not that Valerie expected she would sleep. "I have to wait up for Jessica first."

And when her cell phone rang later and she saw it was David, she let it go to voice mail without a moment's regret, as well as the next three times.…

Valerie wandered to the kitchen window when she heard a car coming down Noah's driveway. She looked at her watch—11:00 p.m.

The vehicle came into view. Not Jessica's car, but a truck she didn't recognize. Floodlights lit up the yard, and she spotted Gideon Falcon. Valerie unlocked the back door as he climbed the stairs.

"Something wrong with your cell phone?" he said as a greeting, stopping in the open doorway.

So. He'd been sent to spy. She crossed her arms. "Not that I know of."

"Getting reception okay?"

"Last I checked, yes."

"Noah's landline working?"

"Yes."

He frowned. "Then you're in trouble."

"Why?"

"David's been calling you for hours, as you must be aware. Everything's good here?" He stepped into the kitchen and looked around.

"Noah's children and my daughter are asleep. You're welcome to check on them."

His brows rose at her snippy tone. "So, the even-tempered Valerie has a temper, after all. My little brother tick you off?"

She walked to the sink and filled a glass of water, not liking how easily he'd figured her out. "You could say that. Were you sent to check on me?"

"Yes, although I didn't get the message until five minutes ago as I was driving home from Sacramento. Does he know what he did wrong?"

"I'm sure he does."

"I'm guessing he doesn't know it made you angry, however."

"He should, but he can be oblivious."

Gideon grinned. "Yes. So, you're waiting to bang him over the head with a pan or something?"

She clamped her mouth shut. Why was she talking to Gideon about David, anyway? She was usually so good at keeping her own counsel. "I don't even want to see him," she said, shocking herself that she'd spoken the words aloud.

Another car made its way down the driveway. "I don't know how you're going to escape it." He looked out the window.

"You mean David is coming *here?*"

"If you'd answered your phone, you would've known that. Never mind. It's the nanny."

Ooh, she hated how calm Gideon was, and how entertaining he thought the situation was.

Jessica breezed in. "Am I late for a party?"

"More like a showdown," Gideon said.

"Please stop. This is private," Valerie said.

The young woman looked from one to the other then shrugged. "I'm going to bed. Thanks so much for filling in tonight, Valerie. And for listening to me."

"Did you make a decision?" Valerie asked, moving closer.

Jessica nodded. She left the room.

"Well, I can guess what that was about," Gideon said. "I imagine Noah will be looking for a new nanny. Again."

Valerie didn't confirm or deny his statement. "You can head home now," she said. "As you can see, everything is under control."

He leaned against the kitchen countertop, his arms folded. "And miss the fireworks? No way."

"I'm not a violent person."

"Good thing. David grew up amid daily battles between our father and his mother. He doesn't tolerate fighting."

"I've noticed he's very patient," she said, grudgingly giving him credit for that.

"That would be news to me. All I know is, he doesn't fight."

Another car approached. "Frying pans are in the cabinet under the cook top," Gideon commented, slanting a look her way, challenge in his eyes.

She heard someone take the steps in a hurry. Then the back door flew open.

David stopped just inside the door. "You're okay."

"Of course I'm okay." She took a sip of water, noticed her hand shook.

"Why didn't you answer your phone?"

Noah came in behind David and nudged him forward so that he could shut the door.

"Your children are fine," she said to Noah. "Jessica just went to bed. I'm sorry you were worried."

"Me? Not me." He and Gideon exchanged a look. "You could've called and let David know all was well."

Gideon raised his hands. "I just got here."

"Did you seal the deal?" she asked Noah, avoiding looking at David.

Noah nodded. Tension filled the room like a snorting, pawing bull getting ready to charge.

"Apparently we need to talk," David said evenly.

"Not tonight." If she could delay until tomorrow, when she was calmer, more in control—

"Tonight. Now," he said. "Either here or outside."

She felt the gazes of all three brothers on her. "Outside."

David opened the door and waited for her. She walked past him and down the stairs, not stopping until she found a spot out of earshot of the kitchen.

"What's going on, Valerie?"

"Like you don't know."

He closed his eyes briefly, as if digging for patience. "I don't know."

"You don't respect me at all. You don't acknowledge me as an adult woman capable of taking care of myself and my child." *Because my daughter wants you to be her daddy. Because I'm stupidly in love with you.*

He frowned. "I do respect you. I do acknowledge that you are competent."

"Then why didn't you let me handle the Rawlings in my own way?"

His jaw twitched. "How did you find out?" he asked quietly.

"Does it matter?"

"I guess not. Valerie, I just wanted to help."

"I retained a lawyer. She was handling everything. I didn't

need your help, David. You had no right to act without discussing it with me."

"Sometimes it takes a man-to-man discussion to get things done."

"Is that what happened?" She clenched her jaw. "You had a *man-to-man* with Senior?"

"There will be no custody question, ever. He won't be pursuing anything beyond occasional grandparent visits."

Relief almost drowned her, rooting her in place. "That was all he was ever going to get."

"You don't know men like Rawling. I do. Whatever your lawyer—Laura, I'm assuming—set up, Rawling and his *team* of lawyers would find a way to tear apart. I made sure he wouldn't."

"Should I thank you? Okay, thank you." Her tone didn't reflect her words. "But you also involved my daughter in a secret, one that caused her a great deal of anxiety. How am I supposed to feel about that?"

"I am sorry for that. I can see it was a mistake."

How could she counter his apology? He'd left her nothing to say. "Maybe I should look for another job." She saw hurt flash in his eyes before he shuttered it, his jaw turning to granite.

"You're never going to find a job that pays as well, that'll allow you to pay off your debts."

Ice ran through her blood. "What do you know about my debts?"

"My company runs a credit check on every potential new hire."

"Why?"

"It speaks to character, Valerie. A lot of companies do it."

She hated that he knew how much debt she had. Hated it.

"Look, you told me about the sexual harassment claim," he said. "I knew it was tough for you to find another job. I'd be maxed out, myself, if I were in the same situation. I didn't hold it against you."

Was he really that dense? He couldn't see how condescending he was being?

"And as long as you're already mad at me," he said, "I guess I should tell you that I had payroll put a direct deposit in your checking account, enough to pay off your debts."

"What? Why? I don't want your—"

"It's a loan, not a gift. You can pay it off with interest, *low* interest. We'll make automatic deductions from your paycheck. You determine the amount."

"Why didn't you talk to me first?"

"I wanted to surprise you. I thought it would make you happy. Bring you some relief."

She had a hard time staying angry about it, since she'd considered asking for a loan herself. It's just that he was so…autocratic.

What a mistake she'd made, getting involved with him intimately while working for him. Yet another gross error of judgment. She should've learned by now.

How could she stay with him?

"You're wrong, you know," she said.

"About which thing?" He almost seemed to sigh.

"I could get another good-paying job. Right here. Jessica told me she's quitting. Noah pays extremely well."

"Noah wouldn't hire you."

"Why not?"

"Because I would tell him not to. He's my brother, Valerie. That counts for a lot." He moved closer to her. "Don't quit."

Tears burned her eyes and throat. As idiotic as it was, she loved him. But Hannah was hoping for something that would never happen. Valerie could deal with the pain and disappointment. Hannah couldn't, shouldn't have to.

"I don't know what else to do," she said finally.

He reached out to stroke her hair. She jerked back. He moved closer, made a soothing sound, touched her cheek for just a moment. "Let's go home."

That tiny touch caused an earthquake of reaction inside her. She ignored it. "Hannah's asleep."

"I'll carry her to the car."

No. Nothing paternal. Not now, not ever. She shook her head. "I'll drive her to school in the morning from here. It's what we planned."

"And heaven forbid we should deviate from a plan."

She took a step back from him, hearing frustration—anger?—in his voice. "I'm not *that* strict."

"Yeah. You are."

That stung enough that she didn't have a comeback. "If you have more to say, say it now. This seems like the time to clear the air."

There was a long pause. "I have nothing to say."

He doesn't fight. Gideon's words rang in her head.

But he could apologize.

Would that make the difference? she wondered. Would that be enough? It didn't change the fact that Hannah would only get hurt if they stayed.

"I'll see you tomorrow." She headed back to the house, jogged up the stairs, ignored Gideon and Noah as she strode through the kitchen, then joined Hannah in bed, where she didn't sleep a wink all night.

David followed more slowly. He shut the kitchen door and faced his brothers.

"You obviously didn't kiss and make up," Gideon remarked.

David glared at him.

"What? Kiss? *What?*" Noah said. "Are you crazy? You got involved with her?"

"It takes two to tango."

"You're her boss," Noah said.

"You think I wanted this to happen?" He kept his voice low, but it shook. "It's the last thing I wanted."

"What's she mad about?" Gideon asked.

"I sort of interfered in some business of hers."

"Sort of?" Quiet descended for several long seconds. "Did you apologize?" Gideon asked.

"No."

"Why not?"

"Because I'm not sorry. I handled something she couldn't handle on her own."

"Are you sure?"

He hesitated. Was he? He thought over his confrontation with Senior Rawling. "Yes."

"Sometimes it's incumbent upon us men to apologize for things we don't think need apology," Noah said. "To keep the peace."

"She was wrong to be angry," David stated, annoyed. "I was protecting her. And her daughter. They're in my charge." He saw his brothers exchange looks. "Well, they are. You would've done the same thing."

"Doubtful," Gideon said.

"Yeah," Noah agreed.

They were playing with him, but he wasn't in the mood for it. "Oh, shut up."

Both men laughed.

He walked out.

David wished he'd driven the Falcon. He needed to put the top down and feel the cold October air against his face. He yearned for the feel of the powerful two-seater under him, zipping along the straightaways, taking the curves, tight and fast. He wished he could get lost.

But since he'd taken Noah and their just-in-case suitcases to L.A. with him, he'd had to bring the SUV, so he drove straight home, garaged his car and went upstairs to let Belle out. At least someone was happy to see him.

He followed her downstairs, turned on the pool lights, then sat in a lounge chair. Belle trotted over, laid her head in his lap and nosed his hand.

"How was your day?" he asked, scratching her ears. She wagged her tail. "Mine was good for a while. Then it wasn't."

His gaze landed on the dark cottage. After a minute he walked to it, unlocked the door and stepped inside. Belle didn't wait for him to flip the lights on but went directly to Hannah's room. When she returned a few seconds later she whimpered.

"I know how you feel," he said, standing in the middle of the great room, his hands in his pockets, the emptiness bombarding him. "I don't see how she can be mad at me for protecting her, do you? Isn't that the job of those who are stronger? To protect the weak?" He sighed. "She wouldn't like being called that, weak. She's not. She just can't handle a man like Senior. Shouldn't have to."

David sat on her sofa and opened a photo album sitting on the coffee table. Hannah, from the day she was born, to this year's school picture. The photographs were taken in a variety of settings, many of them apparently places where they'd lived, small, orderly rooms filled with ancient furniture. From garage sales, maybe? Thrift shops?

Hannah smiled in every picture. In a few, she posed in a tutu. In those shots she beamed. He smiled back.

He set the album aside, wandered into the kitchen, opened the refrigerator. Spotless, and filled with healthy foods many in plastic containers, labeled and dated. He peered at one, spaghetti and meatballs, made just the day before. He remembered how good it tasted. The freezer held mint-chip ice cream.

Belle trailed him into Hannah's room, the walls decorated with posters of ballerinas. He didn't know anything about that world and guessed they were famous dancers. She was young to have such a big dream. He wished Valerie would let him pay for lessons. To delay meant—

He shut down the thought. Her daughter. Her choice.

The door to the adjoining bathroom was open, and he went in there next, could smell perfume or soap, he didn't know which, that fruity fragrance he'd never quite identified on

Valerie. Something feminine and heady. Then he continued into her bedroom.

Neat as a pin. She hadn't added anything but a couple of framed photos on the dresser. He moved to look out the window and realized he could see the pool area clearly now that the plants were tamed. He'd swum in the nude many times since she'd come. Had she known? Had she watched? Looked away?

"Belle, come," he ordered quietly. They went up to the house, headed for the staircase to his bedroom. He stopped at the family picture wall, focused on a photo of his father. "You messed me up, big-time," he said, jabbing a finger against the glass. He found the one of his mother. "And you, even more."

An ache settled in his chest as he climbed the stairs. He glanced at the bed. Had it been only this morning that he'd woken up with Valerie, sated and content? What a difference a day made.

He didn't bother to get undressed. He wouldn't sleep.

Belle walked to her doggy bed but didn't lie down. She barked once.

"I know. I'm confusing you. Sorry."

Sorry. Such a simple word. Why couldn't he tell Valerie he was sorry he interfered? He'd apologized for making Hannah a conspirator. Why was the other so difficult?

Was Noah right? Should he just keep the peace, no matter what? Is that all it would take? He knew what would happen if Valerie left. His life would descend into chaos again, even without all the trips to Europe. He'd be sleeping single in a king-size bed once more.

His life.... He shoved his hands through his hair. His *entire* life would revert to the old ways.

And if he apologized? What then? Peace. Order. Valerie in his bed, in his arms. Hannah dancing around the pool, making Belle happy, making everyone smile.

After a few seconds of staring at his empty bed he retraced

his steps. He dragged a dining room chair into the hall, placed it where he could see the photos of his mother and father, and then carried on a long debate with them, getting a lot out of his system, comparing himself to his father, comparing Valerie to his mother.

Then he analyzed Valerie, dissected their every conversation. He looked beyond his appreciation for her as a housekeeper and assistant to the woman at her core. He dug into his own soul, was honest about himself *with* himself, the most honest he'd ever been.

By morning he knew what he had to do. And it didn't involve apologizing.

Chapter Nineteen

"Mom?"

"Hmm?" Valerie pulled up at Hannah's school the next morning. She was exhausted and trying not to show it.

"Please don't be mad at me."

Valerie loosened of her grip on the steering wheel to put her hands on Hannah's shoulders. "I'm not mad at you. Why would you think that?"

"You're not talking to me." Her eyes welled. "I promise I won't keep a secret again. I promise."

"You did nothing wrong, sweetie. Absolutely nothing. I'm just really tired this morning, that's all. I'm sorry you thought I was mad. I'm not."

"Are you mad at Mr. Falcon?"

How could she answer that? "We talked it over last night. It's okay."

"You're not going to quit, are you?"

"Oh, Hannah." She couldn't lie to her daughter, couldn't

tell her that they would be staying, when she didn't know that for sure herself. "I can't promise something like that. Life is full of surprises."

Hannah searched Valerie's eyes. "Did Mr. Falcon talk to my grandparents, like he said?"

"Yes, he did. Everything is fine now. You'll only visit when you want to, and for how long you want to."

"Okay." Her relief roared through with the force of a tsunami. "Mr. Falcon is so nice."

"Yes, he is."

"I like it there, at his house. It's home, you know?"

Valerie gathered her close. "You have a good day." She watched her beautiful daughter until she was safely in the building, then, emotionally drained, headed for Laura's office, having called her earlier.

"You have news?" Laura asked as Valerie took a seat.

She filled Laura in on what David had done. "He decided on his own to handle everything with the Rawlings. The upshot is that there will be no custody issues, not now, not ever."

"What'd he do?"

"He didn't share the details, but he implied I shouldn't worry my pretty little head about it."

"That annoys you," Laura said.

"I'm glad it's taken care of, but he went behind my back to do it. He even involved Hannah."

"David isn't known for patience. He's action oriented, solution oriented."

"I'm learning that."

"Valerie, you know that David's mother left when his parents divorced, don't you?"

"He told me. My father did the same thing, although I was barely two. So?"

"Right. No wonder you're both so pigheaded," Laura said, sitting back.

"Geez, Laura. Just when I'd come to like you."

Laura never took her eyes off Valerie. "His mother abandoned him. Your father abandoned you. Hannah's father abandoned you, too, or so you thought. Neither you nor David will admit you need each other, because you're scared. And pigheaded."

"I don't need you to—"

Laura put up a hand. "I've had a lot of experience with this in my practice, and here's what I've learned. People who've been abandoned have a hard time forming primary relationships. It's a little different for you because you have a child, which is your primary relationship, but how many serious boyfriends have you had since Hannah was born?"

"None," she admitted quietly.

"Why?"

"I never really trusted anyone to—"

"To stay," Laura said, finishing her sentence. "Right? You figured they would leave."

After a moment Valerie nodded.

"David feels like that, too. If a relationship gets serious, he's outta there in a flash."

"We don't have a relationship."

"Don't insult me."

After a moment Valerie stood. Laura followed suit. They shook hands. "Thank you for everything, Laura."

"You're welcome."

Valerie wanted to suggest lunch sometime, but couldn't decide if she wanted a friendship with a woman David had been intimate with. Wouldn't that be too weird?

She left Laura's office and headed toward her car, then saw Dixie coming toward her, not looking like a happy bride-to-be should. In fact, she started crying the moment Valerie said hello.

"What's wrong?" Valerie asked, alarmed.

"Joey."

"Is he hurt?"

"He won't set a date." She pressed her fingertips to the corners of her eyes, then straightened up and shook her head, her hair dancing. Her expression changed from hurt to angry. "I don't know what I expected. He's stalled all these years until he knew I wouldn't take much more. Now it's a new stall."

"What's he afraid of, do you know?"

"No. It's a McCoy family curse affecting the males only. His sisters are all married, but he and his brothers won't commit. I don't get it. His parents had a happy marriage, were good role models. My parents have a good marriage. He shouldn't be gun-shy."

"How much slack are you going to give him?"

"Not much." She looked at her watch. "I'm late for work. Thanks for the shoulder."

"Anytime." Despair gripped Valerie. If Joseph and Dixie couldn't make it, who could? What would David say about it? "See?" It wouldn't take more than that one-word question. He'd be right. One more nail in the marriage-and-family coffin.

Her stomach in knots, she pulled into the garage later, relieved to see David's truck was gone, therefore so was he. She'd just walked into the cottage when her cell phone rang. Senior. Great. Just what she needed.

"Hello?"

"I didn't appreciate your sending your henchman after me. We could've solved this between us."

Valerie dropped onto her sofa and tossed her purse aside. "Not to my satisfaction, I think. And you've got some damage to undo. Hannah told me she overheard you and Mrs. Rawling discussing her. It scared her. I'm not sure she's going to be comfortable with you now."

A beat passed. "I didn't know that. Wait. Hold on."

He covered the mouthpiece and spoke with someone, then Mrs. Rawling came on.

"Valerie, dear, you have my word that we won't interfere.

It was a dream, that's all. The dream of parents who wished for their son back. You don't have anything to fear from us. And we'll make sure that Hannah knows it."

Valerie believed her. "That would be good."

"We'll call later to arrange another visit."

"All right."

"I have to say, I'm really going to miss your mother. She was an excellent housekeeper all these years. But it's probably for the best."

Valerie was shocked but didn't want to let on that her mother hadn't spoken to her. She hung up, waited a second then called her mother.

"So, what's new?" Valerie asked. "Quit any jobs lately?"

"How did you hear? It just happened twenty minutes ago."

Valerie wanted to keep the conversation light, not rock the already shaky boat. At least her mother was talking to her. "It's in the ethers. So, tell me about it."

"It's Mrs. Cullen, do you remember her? She's asked me for years to come work for her. This seemed like the right time. I needed a change. You were right, you know. The kind of natural competition for Hannah between me and the missus wouldn't have been healthy for any of us. But you were wrong when you said it didn't seem to matter if I saw you or my granddaughter. It does matter. Maybe I haven't been good at showing it."

Relief made Valerie go weak. "We'll all make a better effort, then. I miss you, Mom."

"As soon as I'm settled, maybe you'll come for a visit?"

"Yes." They talked a little longer. Although Valerie was grateful for the shift in their relationship, she didn't confide about her relationship with David. When she hung up she debated whether to go up to the house and see what needed to be done.

See if he left her a note or something...

The rumble of his truck pulling into the garage paralyzed

her. She panicked. She could hardly catch her breath, her heart thundered so loud.

Would he come to her? Continue their discussion? Had he thought about it overnight and decided she should leave, after all? That she was complicating his life way too much?

Her hands knotted together, she waited. And waited. And waited. He never came. Never knocked on her door.

When she couldn't stand it any longer, she left the cottage. The moment she saw the yard she stopped. There were pots of purple flowers everywhere, pansies mostly, but mums and asters and some she couldn't identify. She stood and stared, then she saw David on the kitchen deck, watching her.

"You're crazy," she called up to him.

"Maybe. Probably."

Her throat ached. "Is this your way of apologizing?"

"No."

She didn't know whether to laugh or cry, so she groaned in frustration. She'd hoped he would make her decision easier. He hadn't.

"Don't move. I'm coming down," he said. Within a few seconds he was standing in front of her. "I had a sleepless night," he said. "One filled with revelations. I exorcised ghosts. I faced my own demons."

He gestured toward the garden. "And this is the result. This is not my way of apologizing but of telling you I love you."

Was there a word stronger than *stunned? Shocked,* maybe? *Staggered?* She put her face into her hands.

"It's my way of saying please stay," he said, his voice rough and yet so tender, emotion spilling out of him, drifting over her.

He was saying some of the words she wanted to hear, but not all. She was tempted to let it go, but she thought it would set a precedent between them, one where he would always dominate, not include her as a partner. She put her shoulders back. "You're not going to apologize?"

"I didn't do anything wrong. I love you, Valerie. I will protect you with my life. That means sometimes I'll do things you won't like, but they'll always be for your own good. For your protection."

She laughed shakily, coming to more of an understanding of where he came from, where he stood, what his personal rules were. "That's some ego you lug around with you," she said, making light of things because she wanted more from him, much more, and was afraid to show it.

He waited. She finally slipped her hands into his. "I love you, too."

He squeezed her hands almost to the point of pain. "You'll marry me."

There. The magic words. Joy burst inside her. "Yes. Oh, yes."

He kissed her, a deep, lingering merging, warm with promise. "You'll let me adopt Hannah," he said against her mouth.

All her dreams were coming true at the same time. She nodded, her eyes filling. "Hannah seems to think you would make a good father."

"I happen to think she's right. I love that kid. She snuck into my heart. I can't tell you when, but it happened. I think I'd like to have a couple more." He drew a long breath. "That's another revelation I had during my sleepless night."

"I didn't sleep, either." She couldn't stop smiling.

"How fast can you put together a wedding?"

She toyed with the top button of his shirt. "I'm pretty efficient, you know."

"I've learned that."

"But you told me not too long ago that people should know each other better, longer, before they get married. Did you change your mind?"

"Yeah." He brushed her hair from her face and pressed gentle kisses all over her face, leaving her wanting, not satisfying her need by kissing her lips. "When it's right, you know it. A wise woman told me that love conquers all."

The distinctive sound of the school bus approaching made them move apart. There was no time to celebrate by making love. Later, though. Tomorrow, the first of thousands of tomorrows.

He took her hand. "Let's go tell our daughter."

* * * * *

Don't miss the next book
in the WIVES FOR HIRE *series*
THE SINGLE DAD'S VIRGIN WIFE
this October from Silhouette Special Edition.

*Ladies, start your engines with a sneak preview
of Harlequin's officially licensed
NASCAR® romance series.*

Life in a famous racing family comes at a price

All his life Larry Grosso has lived in the shadow of his
well-known racing family—but it's now time for him to
take what he wants. And on top of that list is Crystal
Hayes—breathtaking, sweet…and twenty-two years
younger.But their age difference is creating animosity
within their families, and suddenly their romance is the
talk of the entire NASCAR circuit!

*Turn the page for a sneak preview of
OVERHEATED
by Barbara Dunlop
On sale July 29 wherever books are sold.*

Rufus, as Crystal Hayes had decided to call the black Lab, slept soundly on the soft seat even as she maneuvered the Softco truck in front of the Dean Grosso garage. Engines fired through the open bay doors, compressors clacked and impact tools whined as the teams tweaked their race cars in preparation for qualifying at the third race in Charlotte.

As always when she visited the garage area, Crystal experienced a vicarious thrill, watching the technicians' meticulous, last-minute preparations. As the daughter of a machinist, she understood the difference a fraction of a degree or a thousandth of an inch could make in the performance of a race car.

She muscled the driver's door shut behind her and waved hello to a couple of familiar crew members in their white-and-pale-blue jumpsuits. Then she rounded the back of the truck and rolled up the door. Inside, five boxes were marked Cargill Motors.

One of them was big and heavy, and it had slid forward a few feet, probably when she'd braked to make the narrow parking lot entrance. So she pushed up the sleeves of her canary-yellow T-shirt, then stretched forward to reach the box. A couple of catcalls came her way as her faded blue jeans tightened across her rear end. But she knew they were good-natured, and she simply ignored them.

She dragged the box toward her over the gritty metal floor.

"Let me give you a hand with that," a deep, melodious voice rumbled in her ear.

"I can manage," she responded crisply, not wanting to engage with any of the catcallers.

Here in the garage, the last thing she needed was one of the guys treating her as if she was something other than, well, one of the guys.

She'd learned long ago there was something about her that made men toss out pickup lines like parade candy. And she'd been around race crews long enough to know she needed to behave like a buddy, not a potential date.

She piled the smaller boxes on top of the large one.

"It looks heavy," said the voice.

"I'm tough," she assured him as she scooped the pile into her arms.

He didn't move away, so she turned her head to subject him to a *back off* stare. But she found herself staring into a compelling pair of green…no, brown…no, hazel eyes. She did a double take as they seemed to twinkle, multicolored, under the garage lights.

The man insistently held out his hands for the boxes. There was a dignity in his tone and little crinkles around his eyes that hinted at wisdom. There wasn't a single sign of flirtation in his expression, but Crystal was still cautious.

"You know I'm being paid to move this, right?" she asked him.

"That doesn't mean I can't be a gentleman."

Somebody whistled from a workbench. "Go, Professor Larry."

The man named Larry tossed a "Back off" over his shoulder. Then he turned to Crystal. "Sorry about that."

"Are you for real?" she asked, growing uncomfortable with the attention they were drawing. The last thing she needed was some latter-day Sir Galahad defending her honor at the track.

He quirked a dark eyebrow in a question.

"I mean," she elaborated, "you don't need to worry. I've been fending off the wolves since I was seventeen."

"Doesn't make it right," he countered, attempting to lift the boxes from her hands.

She jerked back. "You're not making it any easier."

He frowned.

"You carry this box, and they start thinking of me as a girl."

Professor Larry dipped his gaze to take in the curves of her figure. "Hate to tell you this," he said, a little twinkle coming into those multifaceted eyes.

Something about his look made her shiver inside. It was a ridiculous reaction. Guys had given her the once-over a million times. She'd learned long ago to ignore it.

"Odds are," Larry continued, a teasing drawl in his tone, "they already have."

She turned pointedly away, boxes in hand as she marched across the floor. She could feel him watching her from behind.

* * * * *

Crystal Hayes could do without her looks,
men obsessed with her looks and guys who think
they're God's gift to the ladies.
Would Larry be the one guy who could blow all
of Crystal's preconceptions away?
Look for OVERHEATED
by Barbara Dunlop.
On sale July 29, 2008.

HARLEQUIN
More Than Words

"There are moms. There are angels. And then there's Sally."

—**Kathleen O'Brien,** author

*Kathleen wrote "Step by Step," inspired by Sally Hanna-Schaefer, founder of **Mother/Child Residential Program**, where for over twenty-six years Sally has provided support for pregnant women and women with children.*

Look for *"Step by Step"* in
More Than Words, Vol. 4,
available in April 2008 at eHarlequin.com
or wherever books are sold.

⚓ HARLEQUIN

SUPPORTING CAUSES OF CONCERN TO WOMEN
WWW.HARLEQUINMORETHANWORDS.COM

MTW07SH2

REQUEST YOUR FREE BOOKS!
2 FREE NOVELS PLUS 2 FREE GIFTS!

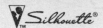

SPECIAL EDITION®

Life, Love and Family!

YES! Please send me 2 FREE Silhouette Special Edition® novels and my 2 FREE gifts (gifts are worth about $10). After receiving them, if I don't wish to receive any more books, I can return the shipping statement marked "cancel." If I don't cancel, I will receive 6 brand-new novels every month and be billed just $4.24 per book in the U.S. or $4.99 per book in Canada, plus 25¢ shipping and handling per book and applicable taxes, if any*. That's a savings of at least 15% off the cover price! I understand that accepting the 2 free books and gifts places me under no obligation to buy anything. I can always return a shipment and cancel at any time. Even if I never buy another book from Silhouette, the two free books and gifts are mine to keep forever.

235 SDN EEYU 335 SDN EEY6

Name	(PLEASE PRINT)	
Address		Apt. #
City	State/Prov.	Zip/Postal Code

Signature (if under 18, a parent or guardian must sign)

Mail to the Silhouette Reader Service:
IN U.S.A.: P.O. Box 1867, Buffalo, NY 14240-1867
IN CANADA: P.O. Box 609, Fort Erie, Ontario L2A 5X3

Not valid to current subscribers of Silhouette Special Edition books.

Want to try two free books from another line?
Call 1-800-873-8635 or visit www.morefreebooks.com.

* Terms and prices subject to change without notice. N.Y. residents add applicable sales tax. Canadian residents will be charged applicable provincial taxes and GST. Offer not valid in Quebec. This offer is limited to one order per household. All orders subject to approval. Credit or debit balances in a customer's account(s) may be offset by any other outstanding balance owed by or to the customer. Please allow 4 to 6 weeks for delivery. Offer available while quantities last.

Your Privacy: Silhouette is committed to protecting your privacy. Our Privacy Policy is available online at www.eHarlequin.com or upon request from the Reader Service. From time to time we make our lists of customers available to reputable third parties who may have a product or service of interest to you. If you would prefer we not share your name and address, please check here. ☐

SSE08R

Silhouette *Desire*

LAURA WRIGHT

FRONT PAGE ENGAGEMENT

Media mogul and playboy Trent Tanford is being blackmailed *and* he's involved in a scandal. Needing to shed his image, Trent marries his girl-next-door neighbor, Carrie Gray, with some major cash tossed her way. Carrie accepts for her own reasons, but falls in love with Trent and wonders if he could feel the same way about her— even though their mock marriage was, after all, just a business deal.

**Available August
wherever books are sold.**

Always Powerful, Passionate and Provocative.

COMING NEXT MONTH

SSECNM0708